THE WOLF AND THE NECROMANCER

A SAPPHIC PARANORMAL ROMANCE

DEFOLF PACK SERIES

LUCILLE YATES

Kitty Hex Press

www.lucilleyateswrites.com

DEDICATION

To my mother-in-law.

Thank you for supporting me, acting as a beta reader (you find all my misused homophones), and wanting to discuss the sexy time scenes with me (even when it's weird).

CHAPTER 1

Tessa

"The alpha is dead."

I stared at my phone, not hearing anything after that. So many thoughts and questions floated in my mind, and I couldn't put any of them into words. The sounds of typing stopped around me.

"You okay, boss?"

I looked up at my employees. "He's dead."

"Who?" someone asked from the back of the room.

"My father."

Murmurs broke out across the room.

"The alpha died?"

"How?"

"Who's in charge now?"

"Oh god, I hope it's not Blake."

I stood up and walked toward the exit. "Y'all, listen to Veronica. She's in charge."

"Veronica doesn't work here anymore."

"Fuck." I closed my eyes and took a deep breath.

"Colt. Colt's in charge."

Tessa

The drive back to the Defolf Pack land went by in a blur. I parked at the two-story building which sat at the entrance of the pack land. It welcomed all and served as the first line of defense. Any visitors of the pack stayed here. The pack held all holidays, ceremonies, and meetings in this building. And, until recently, it was where our father lived. No other leader before him lived in the pack house.

The building resembled a large log cabin. It had two floors plus a basement, with space to host up to eight guests. According to the pack elders, the pack hadn't had guests since our father took over. He held a deep distrust of anyone outside of the pack, especially humans. He claimed they smelled wrong. I suspected there was a story behind it, but he'd never shared it with anyone.

My youngest brother, Lucas, sat on the steps of the pack house with tears streaming down his face. My second to the youngest brother, Blake, stood on the porch in a heated exchange with one of the pack elders, Nico. Lucas ran to me when I stepped out of the car, throwing his arms around me, clinging to me. Flynn, the second oldest, left years ago. He might return for the funeral, but I wasn't holding my breath.

I smoothed Lucas's hair and said, "I know. Let it out." We walked up the steps as Blake scoffed.

"You're an adult, for God's sake," Blake sneered. "Pull yourself together, Lucas."

Nico grabbed his shoulder and pushed him inside.

The walk to the front door weighed me down. With our father gone, one of us would be the next Alpha. He never told us who he'd named. For the past two hundred years, the Curran family maintained the Alpha status of the Defolf Pack. With four heirs, it wouldn't change today.

If he named anyone but Blake, the pack would change for the better. We'd over turn the xenophobic rules and release the stifling grip on the pack as a whole. However, with Blake in charge, pack life would get worse. Blake used fear and pain to his advantage. The Defolf Pack would probably fall, the Curran name tarnished within the shifter community.

Lucas pulled away from me before we stepped through the door. "Tessa, I want you to be the next alpha."

I gave him a soft smile and guided him through the door. The only thing I knew for certain was that my name would not be called.

Tessa

"I can't believe he died," my best friend Veronica's voice came over the phone. "He wasn't the nicest guy. You sure this wasn't an attempt at mutiny?"

I laughed despite myself. "Maybe, if we lived on a

boat and not in the mountains of North Georgia. I think the word you're looking for is coup."

"Same thing." I could almost hear her roll her eyes. "You don't sound sad."

"I am sad. But it feels like I lost a boss and not a father. Maybe a distant family member? He never really acted like my dad. He was more of a ruler."

"Lucas is probably devastated."

"He is. He was the one father spoiled."

"Poor Lucas. Fuck, this entire situation is nuts. Your dad died young. He was around sixty, right?"

"Yeah. But shifters can live for a long time. I didn't expect him to die for another fifty years or die from fighting another shifter or falling out of a tree or something equally stupid."

"And he didn't name an heir. Are you sure the psychic you're going to is legit? I mean, you can't be sure she's an actual witch. Is there an approved list of...real witches?" The uncertainty in her voice made me laugh. Veronica might be related to shifters, but she herself was human.

"No. There is no list."

"Well, good luck. I hope they can communicate with your dad long enough for him to name an heir. Damn. Drama follows your pack."

"Still glad you left?" I spoke with Veronica over Bluetooth as I drove to my appointment with the psychic.

"I was never glad to leave."

"I'll give you a raise if you come back." I said in a singsong voice. Veronica was my best coder, my right-hand woman, and helped me develop our moneymaker Shift&Mate, an online dating app that could filter the paranormal community away from humans. Of course, there was an option to date humans that only ten percent of the paranormal applicants chose.

She left her job at my company and moved hours away. I guess she got tired of working with shifters. Not like she could get away from us. She had shifter cousins. There had to be more to it.

"I can't. I have my reasons."

"I wish I knew those reasons, even if it is, 'Tessa, you're a terrible boss,'" I said. If only I could shake her.

I heard her sigh. "So the whole alpha business will be taken care of in a few hours?"

"Yep. I just parked in front of the shop. I'll call you when the new alpha is named."

"Okay. Love ya, T."

"Love ya, too V."

★ ★ ★

Penelope

The stack of bills looked more like a book than anything else. I laid my head down on top, hoping I could magic them away. As a witch, shouldn't I be able to erase all my debt?

It wasn't even my own debt. I could pay my expenses most of the time, but I couldn't cover my mom's medical bills, too. Even with insurance, the total was more than the cost of my car. The doctor's hadn't cleared my mom to work full time yet, not that it mattered. Disability leave only lasted so long. Her job was long gone. She had a part-time job at the moment, which helped. Every little bit helped.

She called me earlier to chat and let it slip that her leg hurt. It didn't matter what happened to her, I'd worry over it. She still teases me about how I acted when she had a paper-cut while undergoing chemo. I shook my head. She just slept on it wrong, is what she told me. Nothing to worry about.

"Penelope," Olivia said, poking her head into my tiny office. "Ready to open up?"

I looked up with a sigh. Olivia kept her hair in a bun while she worked. It looked nice and tight right now, but by mid-morning the bun would sag and bits of hair would pull out. It was part of her charm and what some of my customers called the 'hard working look.'

"Yeah." I stood up and smoothed out the front of my dress. "Let's sell some coffee."

CHAPTER 2

Tessa

Across the street from the coffee shop, I watched the steady stream of customers slow down. The shop always looked busy at this time of day, though the crowds would thin out within half an hour.

Espresso Yourself sat on the corner of Johnson and Plum at the edge of the small downtown district, and I came here at least twice a week. I discovered it a few months ago, and it became my go-to spot instantly. The mochas tasted like heaven.

The rich coffee smells escaped the door, helping me shake off my trepidation. Despite my regular visit to the shop, today's visit was not about coffee. Inside the café might be my last hope of finding help for my pack's unique problem. I'd spent a week looking for a witch willing to help. I couldn't walk away. I had to keep going. So much for being solved in a few hours.

The small store held plenty of tables for customers to sit, as well as two separate couches for those in need of a cozier spot. The white and black checkered floor contrasted with the bright blue walls filled with art. Olivia, the lady making the coffee, worked quickly, hair up in a bun, nose long and pointed. She reminded me of myself, a little unkempt, but on task.

I couldn't quite make out the view of the person taking orders, but her light laughter floated to my ears as she spoke with the customers. While tall, I wasn't as tall as my brothers, and so couldn't see over the customer ordering. I tapped my boots on the floor and crossed my arms over my chest. Few customers stayed in the shop this early in the morning. Most grabbed their coffee to go off to work, no doubt, much like me on a normal workday.

The customer finished his order. He walked off to wait, giving me a view of the cashier, Penelope. Her bright red lips smiled at the lady in front of me. Black hair styled in a bob with bangs flowed around her heart-shaped face. Freckles dotted her adorable wide nose, which were only noticeable due to the amount of time I'd spent staring. The best part about visiting this shop was seeing her. My wolf agreed. She panted happily in my head every time we walked into the café.

Stepping up to the counter, I got a full view of her curvy figure wrapped in a red and white polka-dotted fifties style swing dress. A blue apron completed the look.

"Hey, Tessa." She grinned from ear to ear. "Your usual, pretty lady?"

I felt myself relax under her smile. I still remembered the first time I'd walked into the shop. Penelope had worn a similar outfit, much as she does every day, with her signature bright red lipstick. Only then, she'd worn tiny braids that hung just below her jaw.

"Welcome to Espresso Yourself," she said then. "Can I take you home? I mean your order?"

I remembered how her brown eyes widened and the way she'd stilled. The memory always brought a smile to my face.

"Hey, Penelope. Not today. I want to try something different. I'd like a…" I suddenly forgot the order, the one Psychic Sister Celeste told me to use when she refused to help me. I tried not to smile too wide while I pulled the paper out of my pocket. "An Americano[1], no water, one broccoli floret, and a cherry on top."

Her face dropped at my order. My stomach twisted knowing I caused that expression.

"Do you want it with or without ice?"

"Without. Please."

She nodded, then peeked behind me. "It's going to be about ten minutes for your order to be ready."

"Sounds good."

"Well, Tessa. Please take a seat and I'll bring your order to you." One side of her mouth curled up.

I took a seat near the back wall, next to a bookcase, and watched her take care of the remaining customers. Always taking my drinks to go, I never took the opportunity to watch the barista.

---

[1] Americano: Caffe Americano is a single or double shot of espresso diluted with up to sixteen ounces of hot water.

My phone provided a nice prop to hide my curious eyes behind when she looked my way. I often wondered if she flirted with all the customers, slipping up and asking them to come home with her or to sit in her lap. A part of me hoped she only said those things to me.

She bubbled about behind the counter, greeted everyone, laughed at their jokes, and swished her hips back and forth when making change. I loved her colorful Mary Jane shoes with tiny ghosts on the toes.

I could never pull off the retro vibe. I hated wearing dresses, much to my father's dismay. He wanted his only daughter to grow up, find a mate, have pups, and continue the pack. But I'm also the oldest and most responsible. I'd spent more time helping raise my brothers than thinking about dresses and dates. But now he was gone, and the pack was in turmoil. Without a declared successor, sibling war would soon begin. We needed a seer's help, or the next best thing.

Penelope walked up to me and handed me a cup.

"What's this?" I picked it up and sniffed it.

"Your order." She smirked.

"A mocha." I sipped the concoction and moaned. "I was worried you'd give me what I ordered. Your mochas are the best."

"You don't want broccoli in your coffee?" She pursed her red lips together. "I'm glad you like our mochas. I like knowing why people come back."

I put the coffee down and leaned forward. "So that order is supposed to come with a consultation. Is that right? Am I supposed to talk to you?"

"Yes, and yes. You talk to me. Come on. Follow me. We can talk in the back office."

I followed her through the door behind the counter, mesmerized by the sway of her hips. Away from the shop floor, I realized she smelled like the mocha in my hand. I shook my head and reminded myself to stay focused. She led me to a small room equipped with a desk piled with papers, a filing cabinet, and two chairs. She closed the door behind me and took a seat, motioning for me to do the same.

"So, Tessa, what brings you to my lap? I mean cafe today?" A slight flush of red appeared across her nose for a second.

I smiled at her slip up. Surely, she did it on purpose. "I need to talk to my father."

"When did he pass?"

"A week ago."

"I see. And how did you get my information?"

"Sister Celeste sent me."

She raised an eyebrow. "Why wouldn't she help you herself?"

I dreaded this question. It sent me down the road where she'd also deny my request. I sighed. "No other witch will help me. I think Celeste gave me your information out of pity."

She blinked at me and looked around the room. "Why won't they help you?"

I looked down at my hands. "My father is Jeremy Curran."

Silence filled the space between us. She looked me

over, her hands folded in her lap.

A hush fell over the room, and the air thickened. It felt like breathing in smog in a major city. The hair on my arms stood on end. Sweat trickled down the back of my neck. The atmosphere reminded me of my previous visits to the various seers over the last week.

After a few minutes, the air would return to normal. That's what happened when I met with the other seers. Except Sister Celeste. The air stayed heavy the entirety of our conversation.

Her small shop smelled of jasmine instead of the lavender of the other seer's abodes. Half of Sister Celeste's white hair was pulled away from her face, the rest fell over her shoulders, reaching her waist. Light brown eyes saw straight through me. She instantly knew why I came to her. After sitting down in the increasingly stuffy room, she grabbed my hand and peered into my very soul.

Sister Celeste said, "You don't know why we won't help?"

I shook my head.

The old woman patted my hand. "I'll tell you, young wolf."

I listened to her tale of woe of a witch and her child being hurt by my raging father. My heart ached for the woman and her family. Tears stained my cheeks at the end of her story. She still refused to help me. Though she led me to Espresso Yourself.

I laid awake that night worrying about how Penelope might look at me once she learned about my father. As much as I tried to tell myself that she wasn't the witch Sister Celeste told me to seek, I knew I was wrong.

Penelope stared back at me now, a frown on her pretty lips. The air started to thin. I took a deep breath.

"I know he wronged the witch community all those years ago. I just learned the extent of it yesterday. But he died and didn't name a successor from his four children. There will be a civil war within the Defolf Pack. And if Blake wins, it could mean a spread of terror in the region. I don't know if we can win against him." I didn't like my odds of saving the pack or surviving without knowing exactly how many of the pack followed Blake.

"Tessa, you're one of my favorite customers and your story is… different. Normally, I would help, but I can't help a Curran, especially when it involves raising the man who shunned my community." She stood with a soft smile.

"I'll pay you." I had to do something before my last hope walked away. "Handsomely."

"Handsomely?" She raised an eyebrow and swallowed hard.

"Five thousand."

"Five thousand, to raise your father's spirit?" she whispered.

"Yes." My heartbeat quickened.

She didn't look at me while she slowly breathed in and out. I watched as she pursed her lips and smoothed out the front of her apron with the palms of her hands. Her eyes tracked over to her desk, then gradually back to me.

"Half now?" she asked.

"Half now."

"Deal." She stuck out her hand.

I stood and shook it. A weight lifted off my shoulders. My hand tingled at her touch, like it always did. It might be dangerous working with her. She wasn't an ordinary witch. If what Sister Celeste told me was true, I'd struck a deal with a necromancer, who owned a coffee shop, dressed in retro clothes, and caused the wolf inside me to pant on sight.

CHAPTER 3

Penelope

I sat back down across from Tessa. I tilted my head to the side, taking in the view. Her long brown hair flowed wildly over her shoulders. She wore a plain light blue t-shirt, half tucked into her skinny jeans. Her black ankle boots tapped the linoleum floor in rhythm with the song playing in the background.

I never expected her to be a Curran. While she never said, I had a feeling she was a shifter or connected to the supernatural. I always flashed her my best smile since the day she walked into Espresso Yourself. The small touches from passing cards and cups sent goosebumps up my arm each time. Normally, I didn't hold back when I found someone attractive, but Tessa made me nervous. I could never get the words out of my mouth to ask her out. This would be the perfect opportunity to get to know her better, if she weren't a Curran.

Every witch worth their salt knew about the Defolf Pack. Thirty years ago, the leader Jeremy Curran hired a psychic, Alana Elsher, to tell him about his first unborn child. Alana was known throughout the southeast as the most accurate seer in the last century. Even with keeping a low profile, she pulled in customers from small town farmers to big shot government agents.

Jeremy raged when he learned the child in his wife's belly was female and refused to pay. She let him walk away, but he couldn't leave it alone. He returned that same night and burned down her metaphysical shop, harming her and her son. She cursed him.

The head of the local Witch's Council forbade the witches in the surrounding area to work with or for the family or the pack. The Southeast Witch's Council implemented the same order not long after. Everyone had too much respect for Elana Elsher and too much fear of the Council to disobey.

Tessa must be the firstborn female. Working for her went against the directive of the Southeast Witch's Council, but I couldn't really turn down the money with my mom's medical bills. I couldn't take a second mortgage out on my house because of my business loans. Would the risk be worth it? The Council already held a strong dislike for me and my type of magic, as if I could help it. No one ever told me the consequences of working with the Curran family, and I'd never asked.

Working with Tessa presented a separate set of consequences. Her golden eyes alone sent tingles to my core.

I readjusted myself in the seat. "What exactly do you need? And when?"

"I need someone to communicate with my father, ask him to name the new leader, and it needs to be done as soon as possible."

Her intense stare glued me to my chair. I never wanted to blink again. "How many witches did you visit before me?"

"You're number thirteen. Celeste is the only one who would even do a reading. The rest gave me a refund."

"I have to warn you. I'm not like the others. I'm not a psychic."

"She told me." She swallowed and shrank down in her seat, looking away.

I frowned. I didn't want her to react to me the same way everyone else did. Seeing her smile each week brightened my day. "I'll need something a little different to call forth your father's spirit. I'll need a piece of him."

"A piece of him? Like his flesh?"

I nodded. "His flesh, a bone, some hair, nail clippings. Something of the sort should suffice."

"Well, I guess it helps that he was a little morbid." She pulled a necklace from under her shirt. A white bone, around an inch in length, dangled from the chain. "His will requested that each of his children receive a necklace with a charm made from one of his knuckles."

"I have never seen anything like it." I raised an eyebrow at the charm and kept the slew of questions that came to me trapped behind my lips.

"I'm pretty sure he wants them to be a sort of relic." She scrunched her nose at her inheritance.

"Charming."

"He had his quirks."

"I can be yours." My mouth moved before I could stop it. Again. I shook my head, heat filling my cheeks. "I mean, I'm available this afternoon. The shop closes at two. I can leave here at three."

"The pack territory is about forty-five minutes away. I can give you a check for half when you get there, if that's okay. I'll write down the address. And my number as well." She wrote the information on a pad I handed her.

I nodded. "A check is fine. Make it out to Penelope Solace."

"Thank you." She stood up, shaking my hand. "You don't know what it means for you to help."

I smiled. Her smooth, warm hand felt perfect in my own. After months of brushing fingers when handing her coffee, I regretted letting go of her hand. "No, thank you. Really."

We both moved at once, bumping into each other.

"Sorry."

"Sorry." I laughed. I put my hand on the small of her back and lightly pushed her out of the room. The warmth of her skin spread up my arm. She left the café, and I watched her walk away past the windows. She didn't look back, though I desperately wanted her to.

"She's cute," Olivia said. She worked at the café as a co-manager four days a week. "You finally ask her out?"

"No. Turns out she's very dangerous."

"So you're still planning on asking her out?" She waggled her eyebrows at me.

"Absolutely."

CHAPTER 4

Tessa

My youngest brother, Lucas, paced in front of the pack house. I knew the pack house felt intimidating when driving onto pack land. While only two stories, the house looked enormous and loomed over visitors. Once you passed it, the rest of the property felt welcoming.

Everyone's homes stood beyond the pack house, laid out similar to traditional subdivisions. Roads twisted down through the tall trees to the homes. The roads looped around, connecting to one another and back to the entrance with only one dead end leading to the cemetery.

"Sit down, Lucas," Blake said. He lounged on the pack house's front steps; his dark eyes following Lucas. "This witch Tessa found isn't coming. She's wasting our time, prolonging the inevitable."

"And what exactly is inevitable?" I tilted my head to the side.

"I'm the new leader. We don't need a dead man's

word." Blake brushed off the non-existent dirt from his sleeve.

"Blake Curran," Nico, the pack elder, said. He narrowed his eyes, smoothing out the wrinkles along his forehead. "If the firstborn is not a son, then pack law demands the incoming leader be assigned by the outgoing one. If a new leader is not chosen, then a fight between the next of kin declares the new ruler."

"I know the rules, old man." Blake rolled his eyes.

Nico huffed and walked into the house.

"You sure you haven't found your mate yet?" Lucas asked me as he paced faster. A breeze cut through his blond hair.

I hated it. I'd be the leader if I'd been born a man. The old archaic rules were unchanged for centuries. The only way I could become the leader is if I had someone to bond with, the shifter equivalent of marriage. Preferably with my true mate. Either way, I'd be out of luck. Soul mates were few and far between in our pack. At some point, the leaders banned non-shifters, claiming it created weak offspring. I suspected my father issued that ban. It made finding a mate harder, and I didn't know a shifter I wanted to share a drink with, much less stick my tongue down their throat.

Lucas assumed I'd automatically become the leader if I found my mate. He held romantic ideas of how the pack should run. I knew better. Our father admired brawn over brains. While I had both, Blake had an abundance of muscle.

"I'm sure. I could fake it, but I'm sure Nico here would

be able to tell."

"Do you hear that?" Lucas asked. "Someone's coming."

"Let's meet this fake psychic of Tessa's." Blake stood up, crossing his arms over his wide chest.

"She's not exactly a psychic." I ignored the puzzled looks from my brothers.

Penelope's hybrid vehicle struggled on the broken asphalt leading to the pack house. When her car stopped inches in front of me, she smiled. She stepped out of a car wearing high-waisted capris pants with a black belt, a red striped button-up shirt, and a red bandana wrapped around her head like a headband, tied on top. Her outfit matched her signature cherry red lipstick. I thought the dress she wore earlier accentuated her hips, but the capris stretched over her curves, making my mouth run dry.

"Tessa." She walked up and shook my hand. "Let me get my stuff."

My wolf gave a happy yip inside my head as I followed her to the trunk and handed her a check. "Here's the first half."

She smiled and put the check in her pocket. I reached around and helped with the two black duffel bags she pulled out of her car.

"Thanks," she said with a wink. "Where would you like me to set up?"

Her wink sent heat to my cheeks. "In the backyard of the pack house. Before we go, let me introduce you to my brothers, Blake and Lucas."

Lucas stepped forward and shook her hand. "Thank you for coming."

Blake pushed Lucas aside. He grasped her hand and kissed the back of it. "I never knew witches could be so beautiful."

Penelope snatched her hand away. "It's the glamor. We don't want to run everyone away with our moles."

"I bet your moles are sexy as hell." Blake lowered the pitch of his voice.

"Ew. Boys." She sidestepped and moved beside me. "After you, Tessa."

"This way." Giddy from her reaction to Blake, I led her through the house and into the backyard. Blake followed, red-faced and fist clenched. Lucas snickered, holding up the rear.

The large backyard of the pack house looked empty without the rest of the pack milling about. The playground on the far side of the yard sat empty for the last week of mourning. I suspected it had more to do with Blake running off any children who dared play during the mourning period than anything else. For all our father's many faults, he encouraged the children of the pack to play.

Nico greeted us in the backyard. He walked up to Penelope and gave her a little bow. "I'm Nico Sanchez. I'm the pack elder."

"It's an honor to meet you, Nico." She nodded her head at him. "Where's the best place to set up? Will anyone else join us?"

He motioned to me.

"Anywhere in the backyard is fine," I said. "Let me know if you need anything. There will be a few more people arriving. Is that a problem?"

"Not at all. Though it can upset small children."

"How is a psychic seance thing going to upset small children?" Blake asked, his fists propped on his hips.

Penelope looked at me with wide eyes, then at Blake.

"I told you she's not a psychic."

"Then what the hell is she?" He stomped toward her.

"It's not important." I shoved Blake away from Penelope.

He pushed away from me, though he didn't approach her again. Pack members began to arrive. Some placed a hand on my shoulder. Others offered hugs. All had questions in their eyes. The same questions they'd asked me all week. None of which I could properly answer.

Penelope pulled things out of her bags. First, she pulled out a cauldron the size of a bowling ball, which explained the weight of the bag I carried. Next, she pulled out five candles: two white, two black, and one dark blue. After those followed a glass bottle of water, several pouches, one large crystal, a few smaller crystals, and a lighter.

She set up the candles in a large circle around her, the blue one to the north. The cauldron sat in the middle. All the crystals settled around it. The pouches, six in all, lay in a line outside the crystals.

She moved the bags out of the circle. "Can you grab me a few twigs, please?"

"I'll get them." Lucas took off to the edge of the yard,

scooping up the requested twigs.

"He's full of restless energy these days." I sighed as I watched him. He'd barely sat down over the last week.

"It's understandable. I was the same way when my mom was sick." She watched Lucas work, a frown on her face.

I looked down at her. "Is your mom okay now?"

"Yes. She is. Thank you." Her brown eyes stared into mine.

My heart stopped for a split second. Her teeth tugged at her plump red bottom lip. Her eyes wanted for nothing. After a week of everyone's questioning and demanding stares, it caught me off guard. She already knew her role. She spoke her request. She hid nothing in her expression.

"Here." Lucas put a stack of sticks and twigs in Penelope's arms, breaking our connection.

"Thanks. Once I get the fire in the cauldron going, we can get started. Do we need to wait for anyone else?"

I looked around the clearing. All the families were to send a representative. After a few minutes of going through the crowd, I turned to Nico.

"I think everyone is here. Are we missing anyone?"

"No. Everyone is here."

Penelope pulled me toward the circle.

"Okay. I want the three siblings on the outside of the candles. And your question is, 'Who is the next leader of the pack?'"

"Yes." I sighed.

Her hand wrapped around my forearm and

squeezed. "It'll be alright. I need the bone now."

I pulled the unique necklace off and handed it to her.

With a smile, she walked into the circle. My brothers and I gathered round. She started the fire in the cauldron, then lit the candles. She sprinkled the water around the edge of the circle, then moved to stand behind the line of sachets in the middle. She pulled a pinch of herbs from each of the six pouches at her feet and threw it in the cauldron. The thick smoke smelled like a citrus pumpkin pie. Then she held the bone high in the air.

"I call to thee

Jeremy Curran

Come forth for thy children's call.

Answer the questions

Truthfully

So they may move on.

Come to me, Jeremy Curran."

The air whipped around the crowd, whistling in my ears. Penelope's short black hair whipped around her head. A large white cloud hovered above her.

"Jeremy Curran. You are beckoned," she called again.

The white cloud took the shape of my father. Big and tall, with unruly hair and beard, his wolf wrapped around him in the cloud, still together in death.

His voice echoed over the crowd. "You called a witch? For this?"

His figure swirled around Penelope. She opened her mouth to speak, but he took the opportunity and slid inside her mouth. The wind died down. Wide eyed, Penelope stumbled back, then looked up. My father's eyes stared back at me.

"Whose idea was it to call a witch?" His voice came out of her mouth. "And not just any witch. A necromancer?"

"You hired a necromancer?" Blake yelled at me.

"You called me back. What do you want, girl?" He glared at me, a sneer on Penelope's lips.

"You never declared the next in line. We are on the verge of a war. Tell us now. Who is the leader?" I felt my cheeks burn, but not from embarrassment, from anger. How dare he take over the body of someone else? Even in death, his entitlement persisted. I pushed down the urge to rush into the circle to pull him out of her.

"Where's Flynn?"

I looked at my other brothers. They both shrugged, refusing to speak.

I rolled my eyes. "He is not here. He refused to come home."

"You will get no answer until all four are before me."

"Are you kidding me?" Blake kicked a pinecone into my shin.

"And you. You think I don't know what you've done?"

I looked between Blake and my father. Blake sneered back at him. What did he do?

Penelope's voice escaped. "Get out of me."

"No. I deserve this body more than you," my father's voice rang out.

"You have no idea," she said.

Her body jerked back and forth. I hesitated, wanting to help her, yet worried I'd disturb the circle, causing more damage. Both voices yelled over one another, nothing understandable to my ears. She reached into the small of her back and pulled out a small knife.

"You'll see," she said, and placed the knife on her forearm. In one quick swipe, she cut herself.

I gasped. My father's scream, along with a white cloud, spewed from her mouth. It circled her like before.

"Be gone, Jeremy Curran. Rest. I need you no more." She sliced at the mist with the knife.

The cloud took the form of my father once more, then puffed into nothing. Penelope let out a big breath, then walked to each candle, extinguishing the flame with her finger and thumb. Moving back to the center, she poured the water over the blaze in the cauldron and the cut on her arm, then plopped down on the grass.

"You have your answer. He'll tell you when all the siblings are present."

"You hired a con artist." Blake got in my face. "I don't know how she did it, but you set this up. Hired her, so we'd have to get Flynn back here. You probably want him to be in charge."

"You're insane. If I'd hired her to lie, I would have put Lucas in charge, or even Nico. I don't want this drawn out. I just don't want you in charge." I didn't back down. Our noses almost touched. Murmurs from the pack rose around us.

"Both of you, calm down." Lucas pushed us apart. "We all saw what just happened. We either get Flynn or we go to war. What's it going to be?"

"I'm okay with war." Blake spat at us.

"You're the only one that wants a war." Lucas glared at him.

"I'm the only one who can win one." Blake spat back.

"You don't have as many followers as you think." Lucas shook, red creeping up his neck.

They glared at each other, almost daring each other to make the first move. We all knew Lucas wouldn't start anything, but he didn't dare back down either. I rolled my eyes.

"I'll get Flynn," I said. "You two behave until I get back."

CHAPTER 5

Penelope

The extinguished cauldron fire's smoke drifted into the dimming sky. The last time a spirit possessed my body, I was twelve years old. My chest hurt from the shifter's presence. Jeremy Curran held on to his power in death. Of course, I didn't consider his shifter side. What a rookie move.

I steadied my breathing and focused on the last of the smoke. I didn't even get an answer from him. There goes the money. I really needed it to help with my mom's bills. There was no way I could refuse handing the check back if she asked.

I pulled a cloth from my pocket to clean the cut on my arm. Though only a scratch, it still stung. I dropped my head. The stretch between my shoulder blades helped release tightness and gave me a reason to avoid looking at Tessa. I didn't want to see the disappointment in her eyes.

When did I begin to worry about disappointing

Tessa? Of course, my mom wouldn't approve of me avoiding anyone. She taught me to own up to my mistakes. But the thought of Tessa's disapproval troubled me.

"Own your strengths and accept your weaknesses," my mom would say.

I lifted my head to see Tessa standing over me, her head tilted to the side. She looked the same as she did this morning, only now her long hair hung over her shoulder in a braid. I grabbed the hand she offered, and she pulled me up like I weighed nothing. Her shifter strength caught me off guard.

"Didn't go as you expected?" She rocked on her heels, putting her hands in her pockets.

"No." I dusted myself off. "I haven't had a spirit possess me in twenty years."

"Underestimated the shifter?"

"Didn't even take it into account. I'm sorry, Tessa." I pressed the heal of my hand to my sternum to ease the pressure in my chest.

"Well, assuming I can find my brother, will you come back and try again?" Her eyebrows furrowed over her steady stare.

"You'd really want me to come back for this? After what happened?" I couldn't believe it.

She pulled out another check and handed it to me. The other half of the promised money. "I don't have anyone else. And you didn't exactly fail. He was here. He spoke to us. He just refused to answer the question. I'll pay the same amount again."

I raised an eyebrow. "How long will it take for you to find your brother?"

"Not long. I know where he works. I can have him back here by tomorrow at the latest." Her face fell into a deep frown. "That is, if I can convince him to come back with me."

"Rocky relationship?" I asked before I could stop myself. None of this was my business.

"Yeah. He left because of our dad. I don't know if he'll come back to talk to him one more time."

"Maybe he'll come back for his siblings, if not his dad."

She looked up at the sky. Her lips parted just a tad, drawing me in. My eyes trailed down her jaw to the small dip at the base of her neck. I took a step forward and placed a hand on her arm.

"If you want, I can come with you. I don't work tomorrow." I bit my lip. What a bad idea. She didn't want me to follow her around, and shirking off my responsibilities wouldn't help the coffee shop. Still, I wanted her to say yes. And maybe my presence would help convince her brother to come, guaranteeing me the extra five thousand.

She shook off my hand. "I don't need anyone's help."

"I didn't ask if you needed my help. I asked if you wanted me to go with you."

She paused and stared at me. A stillness fell between us. Despite the small crowd of people in the clearing, I could only sense her. Her golden eyes kept me rooted on the spot. I waited, wanting nothing but her answer. No expectations, but the desire for her to say yes vibrated in the back of my mind.

"Alright, Tessa," Blake said, interrupting the moment. He smirked down at us, his chest puffed out. "I'll come with you. You'll need help."

"No." She pivoted to stand in his space. "Penelope's agreed to come with me."

"The witch?" He sneered at me. "What's she going to do?"

"Keep me company. And not piss off Flynn. We need him back here. Not so mad at you he refuses to come out of spite." She turned away from Blake. "Let's clean this up and go."

With her help, we packed my two bags and dropped them in the trunk of my car.

"Your car will be safe here for the night. My car is at my house. It's a few blocks down, if you don't mind the walk." She motioned with her head toward her home.

Before locking up my hybrid, I pulled out my large black crossover bag. I walked with her down the old asphalt road, past tall trees which hid the sprawling community of homes of the pack members. The houses we passed were built in different styles in a variety of colors, though they all had two things in common. Each one had a front porch large enough for chairs and no one had a fence. None of the houses could compare to the one welcoming people to the pack, but I preferred a cozy, lived-in home.

She told me who lived in each of the houses as we passed and their shifter type, often waving at the owners who stood on the porch. Several met her at the road to give her a hug and whisper something in her ears. I tried to hear their words, but only succeeded in making myself more curious. Her phone chirped constantly on the walk. She didn't seem to realize how much everyone looked to her for answers. She could bring a positive path to her pack and the surrounding community if given the opportunity.

"Are you going to check your phone?" I asked.

"Yeah. When I get to the house. Here it is, the last one on the block."

The single-story home sat back behind two huge oaks. The light blue house had a porch swing and empty planters on each side of the steps leading to the door. As we walked closer, I felt the cemetery before I saw it. The quiet hum of the undead trickled up through my feet, calling me to come closer. It lay roughly thirty yards from her home in a clearing through the trees.

"Not many people choose to live next to a graveyard."

"It never bothered me. And it keeps the more... talkative members of the pack out of my home."

I laughed. "I like the feel of your cemetery. It's peaceful."

She smiled. "I'm glad to hear that."

She opened the passenger side of her red BMW for me. I paused. No one ever opened a car door for me before. I slid into the seat while biting my bottom lip. Something about the way she looked at me made my heart beat faster.

She closed the door for me. Her car smelled like vanilla. When she sat in the driver's seat, she pulled out her phone. The curve of her neck mesmerized me while she read her messages.

"Thank you. I hope you're ready for a brief adventure. He's only about two hours away." She put her phone up.

"Yeah. This will be a pleasant change of pace. Different from coffee shops and gardening."

"Of course you like gardening." She started the car and headed out of the neighborhood.

"Gardening is amazing. You should try it."

"All my plants die. I have a black thumb, I'm afraid."

"That explains the empty planters. You've got to talk to them."

"Oh yeah? What do you tell your plants?"

"That if they don't grow, I'll feed them to the dead."

She laughed. No one ever laughed at that joke.

"Do you threaten other things besides plants? The 'I'll feed you to the dead' part?"

"Usually other witches. They get so nervous around me. Most don't even laugh when I say it."

"Can the dead eat people?" She glanced at me with an eyebrow raised.

"Nah. They can bite. And punch and kick. And at times, they will dance."

"And my dad was the first shifter you raised?"

"Yep. I'll have him dancing before long. You wait."

"I might pay you more to see that."

"It'll be on the house."

CHAPTER 6

Tessa

"So why can't you call your brother?" Penelope asked as I pulled onto the main road.

"He left about ten years ago, because he didn't get along with our dad and he had plans which didn't revolve around the pack. So, dad kicked him out."

"And he didn't leave a phone number?" She angled herself toward me while she asked questions.

"We email back and forth. Sometimes he'll call, but it's always from his work. When I call back, they won't connect me."

"Where does he work?"

"At a hospital about two hours south of here. He's a nurse anesthesiologist."

"Wow. I hear it's a hard job to get. Good for him."

"Yeah. He's happy there. I hate to ask him to come back, even for a few minutes."

"I'm sure he'll understand." She patted my knee with a smile. "You're the oldest, right?"

"Yep."

"Why aren't you the automatic leader? I mean, it's just how the other shifter packs I know do it. It's just the oldest is the leader or the pack votes."

"Our pack has yet to shake off the old patriarchal ways." I squeezed the steering wheel, thinking about it. "The old leader must name the new one if the oldest isn't male. And a female can only become the next leader if she has bonded with another, and this pack prefers the female leaders to bond with their true mate."

"I don't think I've met a shifter who's found their true mate. They are all quite content with the partners they pick. How do you even know when someone is your true mate, anyway?"

"From what I understand, you just know. It could be from a smell or a kiss. Some people know when they see the other person. Every shifter is different, so we all know in different ways." I longed for someone to stand by my side, but I feared who fate had in store for me. I'd reject an overbearing, controlling mate, even at the detriment of the pack. Lucas would never forgive me if that happened.

"And you haven't found your true mate?" She bit her lower lip while picking at the invisible lint on her pants.

"Right. Which means I'm not in the running. My father must name the next in line, only my father died suddenly. Quite young for a shifter, in fact."

"I truly am sorry for your loss." She squeezed my knee. "It's hard to lose someone, more so when it's unexpected."

I appreciated her condolences, even if it didn't feel like I'd lost a father, but a boss. I nodded and paid attention to the road.

It didn't take long for me to notice the peaceful silence in the car. Penelope sat back, watching the trees pass. She pointed out interesting plants along the way and regaled me with facts about any graveyards we passed. She bobbed her head back and forth, like a song played in her mind. The wolf inside me panted happily during the drive, ever present and calm.

"So, you know I own a coffee shop, but what do you do, besides hire witches to talk to the dead?" She turned to me, not hiding her gaze.

"I am the CEO of Shift Top. It's a part of the Defolf, Inc. business. My brainchild come to life. We make phone games and other apps. The most popular being Shift&Mate."

"I've heard of that. It's the dating app for supernaturals. Though I still don't understand how you keep humans off the app."

"We don't. It's an app for everyone. Only you get pushed into the supernatural side if you answer one question the right way."

"What's the question?"

"What's the family name of the bears from Goldilocks?"

Goldilocks and the Three Bears served as a warning to human children to respect privacy, but it held a different meaning when told to supernatural children. It taught supernatural children to be wary of humans.

"Clever."

"See, this means you don't use my app."

"I've never had a problem finding a date."

"Oh, sexy mama here doesn't need technology to find a match." I glanced at her out of the corner of my eye and smirked.

"I'm never looking for a match. I'm looking for a temporary moment of fun with someone else." She stuck out the tip of her tongue as she smiled.

"What if you want more than just a temporary moment with someone?"

"Then I hope they feel the same way."

I looked over at her and smiled. She glanced out the window with a small grin. I admired her open expression and her way of thinking. "And you have tons of people knocking on your door?"

"Sometimes I knock on their door. It's just a matter of if they open it."

"I like it. My new flirting strategy is to open with a knock-knock joke."

She snorted with laughter and slapped my leg. "I love it. Let me know if it works."

My stomach growled over the sounds of the road.

"Are you hungry?" she asked, poking my belly.

"Stop it, witch." I laughed. "And yes."

"Up ahead, there's a little diner to the left. Let's stop there. The food is delicious."

"We really shouldn't stop." I wanted to race to my brother, grab him, and race back. Thoughts of what Blake might do while I'm gone popped up in my mind.

"Your brother will still be there if we're half an hour behind. And, if I'm honest, I'm hungry, too."

I scrunched up my nose. I didn't want to stop, but my stomach growled again.

"They have homemade apple pie," she sang at me.

"Okay. I do love apple pie."

"Yay! Now it's a proper road trip." She lightly bounced in her seat.

I rolled my eyes and turned into the gravel parking lot of the only building in sight. The small brick restaurant had a line of windows in the front facing the road with nothing but wilderness behind it. The sign high over the parking lot read The Old Miner's Kitchen. The illustrated logo contained a small man in an enormous cowboy hat, a pickaxe over one shoulder, and a plate of fried chicken in the other.

"I hope the apple pie tastes better than the fried chicken looks on the logo."

Penelope laughed. "I'll have you know that the fried chicken is so good. I'd even eat it if it looked like the logo."

I smiled and squeezed her hand. "Go ahead and eat it. We're already on our way to the hospital."

CHAPTER 7

Penelope

I moaned as I bit into the apple pie. I loved this diner. I ate here at least once a month, if not more. If I ate here every day, I'd be as big as a house. I opened my eyes to the view of Tessa smirking at me, her eyes laughing.

"What? It's good."

She giggled. "I can tell. You have pie all over your face."

I licked all around my mouth, trying to get it off. She picked up a napkin and leaned over the table. She wiped off the excess, her face inches from mine. Her long lashes emphasized her golden eyes.

"Did you lick me? I mean, did you get everything?" I asked. I felt the heat rise to my cheeks. I thought I had my blunder with words under control.

She licked her lips and smiled. "I got you."

"Yeah. You do."

"Knock-knock," she whispered.

My heart skipped a beat. Her intense stare pulled me

out of myself. It called forth my recklessness. My exhibitionist nature lay underneath, wanting to show the world what I can claim.

I swallowed. "Who's there?"

"Can I get you ladies anything else?" The server pulled us apart with her voice, both of us sitting back in our seats. Busy writing in her pad, the server didn't notice the moment.

Tessa grinned wildly at me; her golden eyes twinkled. I shook my head at her and winked.

"Can I get a coffee to go? Do you want anything?" I looked at Tessa. She shook her head. "And the check, please."

"One ticket or two?"

"One." We both said at the same time.

The server set the bill on the table. Both our hands covered the slip of paper.

"This is going to be interesting," Tessa said.

"Oh, it's already fun." I winked and reached into my large bag with the other hand, pulling out two twenties.

"That's cheating." Her mouth opened in mock shock, then her face fell. She looked over my shoulder out into the parking lot.

"What's going..." I turned to see four large men walk up to the diner. One I recognized from the clearing, from her pack.

"We've got to go. They aren't here for food."

"What?" I dropped the money on the table and grabbed my bag while she pulled me out of the booth.

"Is there a back door?"

"Yeah. Near the bathrooms."

She pulled me out of the restaurant, through the back and out into the forest. "We'll circle back around and jump in the car."

"I don't think I'll be fast enough. I mean, they're all shifters, right?" My heart pounded in my chest. I didn't sign up for a fight.

I ran into her when she stopped short.

"Going somewhere?" a deep voice said.

One man stepped out of the trees in front of us. Tall and slim, scars decorated his face, accenting his crooked nose.

"Yes. I wanted some fresh air before we headed out." Tessa stood still, her stance wide, head cocked to the side.

"We can't let you leave." Another voice said. He appeared to the left. Another came out from the right and I knew the fourth stood behind us.

"Alex, why are you doing this?"

"I have nothing against you, personally. We can't risk someone other than Blake taking over. You understand. This is war."

She looked around the clearing. "This is not war. It doesn't have to be."

"We will not follow Flynn. He's a deserter."

"You don't know that Flynn is the choice."

"Why else would Curran ask for him to be present?"

"My dad is an ass. He used to do this all the time. Once I wanted mom's old bike. We all had to be there when he said I could have it. This is the same thing. Blake might still be the new leader."

"Lies," the man to the right said. "She's afraid to fight."

I looked at her. Her eyes glowed. A growl escaped her throat. My heart felt like it might jump out of my chest at any moment. I wasn't built for physically fighting.

"You're the ones who should be scared." Her hackles rose under her shirt.

I gripped the handle of my bag. I couldn't take on a shifter, and I couldn't outrun one either. What had I gotten into?

"Get 'em, boys," Alex said.

In an instant, all four changed, their clothes shifting with them. I couldn't stop and marvel at the shifting like I normally did. The three I could easily see changed into wolves. The one behind became a bear. Tessa jumped and shifted midair into a large brown wolf with a white belly and snout before plowing right into the wolf named Alex.

The wolf to the left charged me. I swung my bag around, whacking him in the face, then took off toward a tree. Using the skills I learned as a child, I climbed it before the wolf bit my foot. I hit the wolf again in the face. My bag knocked him down on his ass, only a temporary setback until he remembered he could shift and climb after me.

I trembled and watched Tessa take on the other two wolves. The bear didn't fight much, swiping only when she approached. Her jaws clamped around the shoulder of the larger one, bringing him to the ground. The smaller wolf bit her side. Her yelp hit me like a ton of bricks. We had to get out of here.

Rooting around in my bag, I pulled out a small pouch. Magical mace. Not as convenient as regular mace, but less likely to be confiscated. I threw a pinch of the stuff at the wolf jumping at me below. He fell on his back, howling in pain. The two wolves she fought lay on the ground, both tried to get up despite the injuries she'd inflicted. She and the bear circled each other. We had to get out of here. I hit the ground hard and ran toward her, ignoring the sting in my feet.

The bear charged her. I threw the opened pouch at the bear, slid beside her, wrapped my arms around her bleeding torso and took a chance.

"Move us forward,

Move us back

Teleport us

Abeona move us now."

Air escaped my chest when I landed on the gravel between the cars in the parking lot. Tessa's wolf's eyes stared back at me.

"Don't give me that look." I stood up and opened her car door. She hopped in and I sat in the driver's seat.

Grateful for push start technology and the shifter's magical ability to shift with their clothes, I started the car and squealed out of the parking lot. On the seat next to me, Tessa shifted back. Blood dripped down her cheek and onto her leg. Her face looked pale.

"You're losing blood. We need to get you to a hospital."

"No. I heal fast once the bleeding stops. We need to make sure they aren't following us."

It won't matter if she bled to death. I mean, there is a hospital on our way to...the hospital.

CHAPTER 8

Tessa

The pain on my side radiated through my body. It would take some intervention to stop the blood flow, but I didn't want to worry Penelope. I looked behind us. A truck in the distance crept closer.

"Go faster. I think they're in the truck." If they caught up to us, I wouldn't be much help.

She glanced in the rearview mirror and then looked at me. "Are you holding your side? How bad is it?"

"It's not bad, but it needs pressure to stop the bleeding."

"I can't believe they all wanted you dead."

"Everyone but Colt, the bear. Blake has his family hostage. He knows Colt is the strongest fighter in the pack, so he threatened to kill Colt's family if he doesn't help take me out."

"And no one has helped him?" She kept a steady rotation of watching the road, the truck behind us, and me.

"I just found out. Apparently, they are keeping eyes on Colt's little sisters at all times." Blake extorting Colt was low, even for him.

"What do you mean, 'just found out?'" Her wide eyes glanced at me.

"When we are shifted, we can speak to each other telepathically. He told me while we stared each other down."

"Wow. I didn't like Blake before, but I hate him now."

"Join the club. He's a grade A bastard."

"They are almost on our tail. If they drive us off the road, will you be able to fight?"

A bump in the road caused me to cry out from the pain. I'd lost too much blood.

"I'll take that as a no. Hold on. I have a plan. When the car stops, jump out and head for the back of the cemetery."

"I can fend them off. Where is your knife?" I needed to keep Penelope safe. She could run while I fought.

"What knife?"

"The one you cut yourself with when you called my father?"

"That's a ceremonial knife. It's in the trunk of my car."

"Shit." I turned to see the truck approaching fast. My stomach dropped.

"Just run when I stop the car."

"What?" The truck was right on our tail. I saw two different Blake supporters in the cab.

Penelope jerked the car to the right and drove down

a gravel road leading us straight into a cemetery. She stopped in the middle.

"Run." She jumped out with her bag in her hand.

I followed her through the maze of tombstones. I slid in next to her, behind a gravestone.

"I hate to do this." She grimaced and stood up. Her hands stretched out before her, looking larger than life, and she yelled, "Rise!"

The ground trembled around us. I shifted and looked over the top of the gravestone. Blake's men jumped over tombstones toward us until hands reached up and pulled them down. Skeletons emerged from the ground, glowing orange around the joints.

I gasped at the sight. I'd always heard necromancers were dangerous, but I never knew they were so powerful.

Penelope took deep breaths, her hands shaking and lifting higher. "Detain the men." Her voice carried over the large cemetery.

The skeletons swarmed the two shifters. They yelled out in pain from the onslaught. Penelope collapsed to the ground. She used the tombstone to pull herself up and dragged us deeper into the graveyard.

"Where are you going?" Eyes wide, I limped along, holding my side. I could still smell the freshly dug earth behind us.

"Not much further."

She paused at the gate to scatter herbs when we left the cemetery. Then she sprinkled the mixture on both of us. "This will hide our scent and cover our tracks."

The overwhelming scent of frankincense stuck with

me while I followed her through a grove of trees which led us to a small yellow cottage. An old blue pickup sat in the driveway. If we weren't running, I'd stop to admire the picturesque scene of the white lawn furniture and the large willow in the front yard. She pulled us around the house and pushed me through the front door. The small cottage on the edge of the graveyard seemed too good to be true.

At least I had a necromancer on my side.

CHAPTER 9

Penelope

I slammed the door once we made it inside, peeking out the front window.

"Where are we?" Tessa stood next to the love seat and looked around the room.

"This is my place." I leaned against the door. "Can you hand me the bowl sitting on the table there?"

The lively colors of the plush couches draped with afghans and colorful pillows didn't brighten my mood. My magic felt depleted from the strength of the spells I'd cast, like I had a hole in my chest.

Tessa handed me the requested bowl filled with a mixture of herbs strategically placed near the entrance. I took a handful, then blew it onto the door. A gold shimmer flashed from the door outward onto the walls.

"This should shield us for a while. We can't go anywhere until you're healed."

"We have to leave now." She followed me into the kitchen. "We have to get to my brother as soon as possible. If they can't get to me, then they'll get to him."

"You barely know where he is. Do you think they will find him?" I asked. "We need to stop your bleeding so you can heal."

Blood covered her torn shirt. It trickled onto her jeans. I wasn't a healer. What if she bled out?

She looked down. "It's not too bad."

I rolled my eyes and pulled down the first aid kit I kept on top of the refrigerator, along with a bowl down from the cabinets. Once filled with warm water, I carried it, the first aid kit, and a wet towel to the kitchen table. A dry towel draped over my shoulder.

"Let's take off your shirt. We might need to cut it off. I'm sure I can find you something else to wear."

"No, I can take it off." She attempted to lift her shirt, only to cry out and drop her arms.

"Stop." I rested my hand on her arm. "Does this shirt hold any sentimental value?"

She inspected the plain blue shirt. "It's just a shirt."

"Then I'm cutting it off. Hold still."

Once she sat down, I started from the bottom and cut the shirt, pulling it away from her body first. I breathed shallow breaths as I moved up her torso. I kept my motions slow and steady, to keep from hurting her further. This close, she smelled of coffee, vanilla, and blood. When I reached the neck of her shirt, she tilted her head just slightly. Her eyes stared into mine after the last cut. The dip in her skin where her neck and shoulder met called to me. I swallowed hard and helped take off the shirt, exposing her wound and her bare breasts.

The laceration looked bad, but the smaller cuts on her arms began to heal before my eyes. I knelt on the floor in front of her with the bowl of water and cleaned the gash on her side. The teeth marks weren't as deep as I'd imagined.

I focused on her injury instead of the fact she sat in my kitchen wearing nothing but jeans. Or the softness of her skin. I bit my lower lip while I worked. I glanced up to see her take a deep breath and close her eyes.

At last, with a clean wound, I placed a bandage over it, my fingers brushing her skin, sending shivers down my spine. I heard a hitch catch in her throat.

"Oh, sorry." I jerked my hand away. "Did I hurt you?"

"No. Just chills."

"Right. You must be cold, sitting here topless. I'll get you a shirt." I rose with the bowl of water, placed it in the sink, and walked down the hall.

Passing the bathroom on the right, I turned left into my bedroom and opened my drawers. I moved my clothes around, looking for something comfortable for her to wear. She may be taller, but she wasn't much bigger otherwise.

I jumped when I looked up to see her standing before me. I smiled. "I didn't realize you followed me. Here."

She took a step closer, but instead of taking the shirt, she pulled me to her and kissed me. I pushed her off instinctively. My experience with inappropriate customers caused me to act without thinking.

Shocked at my own reaction, I searched her surprised eyes, then pulled her to me and kissed her back.

Our tongues fought for space and possession. My hands roamed over her lean body, grabbing her ass and sinking my fingers into her hair.

She backed me to my bed, both of us falling onto the mattress, never breaking the increasingly desperate kiss. My hands caressed her smooth back, my lips sucked hers. She unbuttoned my shirt with one hand, the other gripped the base of my neck.

"Wait." I breathed hard. "You're hurt. We can't."

"It's healing. I can feel it."

We stared into each other's eyes. She kissed me softly.

"It's fine. I'm healing," she whispered.

"I don't want to hurt you."

"I promise you won't."

I kissed her again and helped with the last button. I rolled us over and straddled her, pulling my shirt off. "This way, you can rest."

She pulled me close, then kissed and nuzzled my neck. Moans escaped my lips. I kissed her neck and nibbled her ear. Fingers dug into my back. She arched into me as I kissed down her front, stopping to tease her nipple. She gasped at the first touch of my mouth on her bare breast. I bit and licked her tight peak. Her hands pulled and scratched my arms.

The way she moaned spurred me on, lapping at her taut nipples. She pulled my mouth back to hers and fumbled with the button of my pants. They dropped to the floor, and her lips found my breast. The cup of my bra pulled out of the way. I gasped and jumped when she pinched my hard bud, but her fingers ventured further down. A single finger slid over the opening of my now drenched pussy.

"You're beautiful," she said into my neck.

"So are you." I escaped her grasp and moved down her torso. Her lovely figure lay on my bed before me. Within a minute, her pants joined mine on the floor and I crawled back up her glorious body. Starting at her knees, I kissed and nipped all the way back up to her plump lips, stopping to rub my face in her clothed mound and to tease her breast once more.

I reached between us and slid my hand under the band of her panties. My long fingers danced through the curls. I rubbed her mound, ever so slightly missing what I knew she wanted me to touch the most. I wanted to tease her, yet didn't want to waste the time we had together.

"May I?" I asked between nibbles of her earlobe.

"Oh yes," she moaned.

One touch of my fingers on her clit sent shivers through her body. I licked up her neck, kissed her lips, and smiled. She tasted like sweat and vanilla. I bit my lip and twitched her pearl, basking in the moan which escaped her.

"Hmm, I like making you moan." I moved my fingers again and sucked on the crook of her neck.

Her hands moved up my back and around, taking my breast in her hands. She flicked my nipples, causing me to buck. Her mouth wrapped around my breast, licking my nipple and flicking it with her tongue. I moaned, and she teased me more, pulling my bud with her teeth. She rubbed her hands down my body, across my stomach, over my hips, then ventured beneath my underwear to grab my ass.

Her hands moved straight to my mound of tight curls. She rubbed my sensitive clit. I gasped and shivered over her. Catching my breath, I looked down into her smiling eyes. My hair dangled down over my face as I held myself with one arm. My other hand rubbed her mound and pinched her bundle of nerves.

She let go of my nipple and kissed me. I kissed her harder and slipped two fingers inside her wetness, my thumb ready on her clit. I kissed down her face into her throat while fondling her nub.

Nibbling her neck, she panted and scratched my back. I loved how she responded to my touch. She arched and rocked into my hand and held on to me with both hands. I moaned into her neck as she rocked faster.

I sucked on her shoulder, tingles going straight to my center as she bucked and rubbed against my sensitive nips. I teased her clit, up and down, left and right; faster, then slower.

She squirmed, moaned and whispered, "Faster."

"Yes, ma'am." I chuckled into her skin.

I rubbed her faster and faster, listened as she panted in my ear. I slowed once more, running my teeth along her shoulder. She whimpered in my grasp, pressing herself harder into my palm.

I gently pressed my teeth into her neck and sped up my movements. Faster and faster, my thumb flicked and teased her clit. She exploded and convulsed under me.

Slowly, I stopped my thumb's movement on her clit. She shivered under me; eyes rolled back in her head. After each buck and twitch, I kissed her lips.

When at last she looked at me, I gave her a Cheshire cat grin. I slowly withdrew my hand from between her legs and winked at her. Her eyes sparkled when I leaned down to kiss her. In the kiss, she rolled us so she could be on top.

"It's my turn to taste you," she said, before closing the distance with a kiss. "Any objections?"

"How's your side?"

"Good enough for me to make you come."

"Then be my guest." I licked her lips and pulled her down into a kiss.

CHAPTER 10

Tessa

Penelope's lips tasted so sweet. I could hover above her and kiss her all day. Right now, however, I had different plans. I sucked on her full bottom lip, then kissed her neck, headed south. I inhaled her scent of coffee and earth as I slowly pecked and tasted my way to her breast.

I admired her matching black and white polka dot bra and panties, though they wouldn't be on her much longer. Using my teeth, I pulled down the cup of her bra and licked her tight nipple. She arched into my mouth, and I slipped my hand under her to unclasp her bra. I pulled the whole thing off and moved to the other nipple.

Flicking and nipping at it with my tongue increased her moans. Her hands sunk into my hair. She stared at me when I looked up at her. I grinned and pulled on her tip with my teeth to watch her gasp. I placed my mouth over as much of her breast as possible, licking away at her glorious tit.

I loved the feeling of her wiggling under me, her soft

skin in my hands. I smelled her arousal increase with each lick of her nipple. With one last kiss to her nips, I continued on my journey to her sweet spot. Each kiss and bite of her skin brought forth a hiss or moan.

Slipping my fingers under the band of her underwear, I pulled them down and off with ease. She offered no resistance as I pushed her legs apart, running my hands up the inside of her soft thighs. Tight, black curls covered her mound. I sank my nose into it, inhaling the deep earth and mocha scent. My fingers trailed down her body, lightly caressing her sides, then grasping her hips. I kissed my way to her glistening vulva. She bucked under me when I flicked her clit with my tongue. I licked it again, then covered it with my lips and sucked on it. She groaned and arched into my mouth.

My hands held her in place so I could explore her further. I licked her clit once more, then moved down to her wet pussy. I tasted her. One lick and my wolf howled inside of me. 'Mate,' she called.

I lapped her up, my tongue reaching into her to get a better taste. My desire for her tripled, masking any shock I might have felt at finding my mate. My hands tightened around her hips as I licked and sucked on her clit. She squirmed and bucked in my grasp. She moaned louder with each flick of her bud, causing me to move faster.

I reached up with one hand and grabbed her sensitive breast. My original plan of taking my time between her legs was now out the window. I pinched and pulled on her nipple while I flicked and rubbed her clit with my tongue. All the while, the word 'mate' echoed around in my head.

All too soon, she shivered and quaked in my mouth. Her moans vibrated with each shudder. I gave her one last long lick, then kissed her sweet vulva. She looked down at me, and I placed my head on her mound.

"You are very good at that." She smiled at me while panting.

"Thank you." I kissed her tight curls and crawled up her body, then laid down beside her. My fingers lightly caressed her side.

She pulled me into a deep, slow kiss, then wrapped her arms around me, pulling me close. I pulled the sheets over us. We kissed and nuzzled our noses together.

"We need to get going." My wolf pranced around inside, happy to be in our mate's arms.

"I need to rest. I used too much magic today. Teleporting and calling forth so many skeletons drained me."

Her dark brown eyes looked into mine. We nuzzled our noses together.

"Okay. Rest. We'll leave in a few hours."

She propped her head up on her hand. Her other hand lightly touched the bandage on my side. "How is your wound? We didn't make it worse, did we?"

I smirked at her. "It's better. Once the bleeding stops, I heal pretty quickly." I pulled back one of the corners of the tape holding the gauze down. Pink skin covered where teeth marks bled less than an hour ago.

Her hand slowly reached down toward the healing wound, but she pulled it back before she touched it.

"Wow. I've never watched a shifter heal before. You should cover it back up, just in case."

I laughed and did what she asked, then pulled her down into a soft kiss. "Time to rest."

She sighed and snuggled into my side. Happy to stay in her arms, I watched her breathing slow as she drifted off to sleep. I worried about what it meant to be mated to a woman. They tolerated homosexual relationships in the pack, but never rejoiced in them like the heterosexual ones. My pack coveted those who reproduced. I could change it as the leader. But would they accept me with a same sex mate? Would I even be considered?

How would they react to my mate being a witch? And a powerful one at that? After decades of pack life with non-shifters, the community might shun me outright.

I brushed the hair out of her face. She looked so small and innocent in my arms, curled into my side. Yet this woman could raise an army of undead. And she was mine. I was hers. Mates.

Would she even want to be my mate? The Witch's Council hated my father and my family name. Could they convince her to reject me? I shook my head.

After a while, I decided it was a problem for future me and fell asleep.

CHAPTER 11

Penelope

At four in the morning, I awoke still wrapped in Tessa's arms. My heart skipped a beat when I looked at her beautiful face. Both gorgeous and strong, I admired the way she took charge of her family and pack. She took the time, spent her energy looking for a way to stop a war between her siblings which would tear the pack apart.

Knowing how the witches viewed her father and his offspring, she risked the embarrassment and rejection to ask for help. Calm and collected, she sought compromise before violence. She also took down two grown shifters alone. A hidden strength underestimated by everyone.

For the first time in my life, I wanted to keep someone for myself. Always content with a little fun, I'd never wanted to pursue anything long term. Now I wanted to try it. Once Tessa received an answer from her father, I'd knock on her door.

I kissed her forehead and untangled myself from her limbs. I pulled out my only pair of exercise pants for her.

It was one of the few pair of pants I had which might be long enough for her to wear. I grabbed the shirt I selected for her the night before, forgotten on the floor, and placed both at the foot of the bed.

I started the coffee pot and jumped into the shower. Wearing my gardening clothes, I made my way to the kitchen after the quick wash. The u-shaped kitchen gave me plenty of counter and cabinet space. A few small pots growing herbs sat on the window seal above the sink. It wasn't quite big enough for an island, but I liked the ease of cooking without dodging furniture. Tessa stood next to the coffee maker, holding a mug of coffee and some papers, only in her underwear. My cheeks heated, and my mouth went dry.

"Good morning." She grinned at me before taking a sip.

I walked toward her and wrapped my arms around her. "Good morning."

She leaned down and gave me a quick kiss. "Who's Tamika?"

I raised an eyebrow, then noticed she held my mother's bills. I pulled them out of her hands and put them in a drawer.

"She's my mom. She had ovarian cancer. She's been cancer free for a year, but the bills are piling up." I didn't tell her it was the reason I agreed to help. Five thousand dollars could go a long way to paying off her bills.

"The Witch's Council won't help?"

"No. My mom's not a witch. My dad was. So they won't help."

She leaned against the counter. "I heard they helped the families of all witches."

I gave her a half smile and glanced down. "They don't exactly like me. Everything they do which involves me is strictly by the books. No deviation. They don't really see me as a traditional witch. They see me as low tier, I suppose." It hurt to be rejected by my kind, even more so for something I couldn't control.

She cupped my face. "They fear you. I've lived with enough power-hungry people to understand what's happening. I saw what you did in the cemetery. If they treat you as less than the rest, they hope you won't see how strong you really are."

I studied her, brows furrowed. Did she really see me as strong?

"Mind if I take a shower?" Her thumb brushed my cheek.

"Go ahead."

She kissed me again before disappearing down the hall.

I fixed myself a cup of coffee and sat at the table. I considered what Tessa told me. Could it be possible the Council feared my power? I saw the truth behind her words. Not everyone understood necromancy. I sighed and put away those thoughts for later.

Now I needed to focus on the next step of our journey. We had to make our way south for another hour, and I hoped her brother was working. My magic felt stronger today. I breathed a sigh of relief. Being magically depleted against a group of shifters wouldn't bode well.

Tessa walked back into the kitchen wearing the clothes I had laid out for her. The outfit looked a smidge tight, but I admired the way she looked in my clothes. She winked at me, then retrieved her coffee from the counter. She sat next to me and watched me as she sipped her coffee. Her golden stare sped up my heart.

"Does your pickup run?" she asked.

"Yeah. We'll take it to the hospital. I can charm the windows so that people will see someone different when they look inside."

"I never knew how handy witches are." She smiled at me. "Thank you for lending me your clothes, by the way."

"Anytime. Besides, you look good in them."

"I wonder what you'd look like in mine." She leaned forward and kissed me deeply.

My mind shut down as I leaned into the kiss, grasping at her hips to keep me steady. I gasped for breath when she pulled away. "What were you saying?"

She laughed and pulled us out of the chairs. "We need to go. Let's get our stuff."

Ten minutes later, we sat in the old pickup truck, riding south. We passed a few suspicious vehicles parked on the roadsides, but none followed us when we passed. I wanted to breathe a sigh of relief, but knew we had a difficult task ahead.

"How many of the pack really support Blake?" I asked.

"Really support him? Maybe five or six members. The rest he blackmails or extorts into supporting him. He's slowly gained a following over the last few years."

I suddenly had a terrible thought. "Do you think...never mind." It wasn't a question I should ask.

"Come on. Just ask."

I looked over then glued my eyes to the road. "Do you think he had anything to do with your father's sudden death?"

She sighed and shook her head. "I just don't know. I really don't know what to think."

"Do you know what you'll say to Flynn when we find him?"

"No. It might be easier to knock him out and kidnap him." She laughed.

"It's only awkward if he wakes up in the cab on the way back." I smirked at her, glancing her way.

She tilted her head against the back glass. "I hope knowing Blake wants to start a war will bring him back."

"Do you think he'll be named the leader?"

"No. He left. My father considered him a deserter. He had a strict view of loyalty."

I squeezed her leg with nothing to say. The cab fell quiet. I held her hand for the rest of the drive with an occasional kiss to her knuckles.

CHAPTER 12

We arrived at the hospital at half past 5. In the quiet morning, few people moved around the four-story white building surrounded by large, full-grown trees.

"Do you know what floor he works on?" Penelope looked through the windshield.

"No."

She sighed. "If he's a nurse anesthesiologist, he'll work in surgery or the maternity ward. Maybe both. Unless he works in the ER."

"I don't think he works in the ER."

"Okay. Surgery is on the first floor. They have an outpatient section and an inpatient section." Her eyes glazed over as she stared at the hospital.

"Is this where...your mom?" I looked away from her and looked out the side window.

"Yeah. She spent a lot of her time here. I know the layout better than I want."

"Do you want to wait here for me?" I squeezed her

knee.

"No." She took a deep breath and shook herself. "Do you see anyone around here we should avoid? Can you smell anyone?"

I rolled down my window a little. A small breeze blew in the surrounding scents. After five minutes, I gave the all clear. If anyone from the pack had found this hospital, they weren't anywhere near this entrance.

We walked into the nearly empty hospital and followed the signs to surgery. We passed a few nurses down the narrow white halls who didn't give us a second glance. We came to an intersection with one arrow pointing toward out-patient surgery and the other to surgery. I looked down at Penelope.

She frowned. "Split up?"

"Yeah."

"What does he look like?"

"Tall, dark short hair, golden eyes, and he glides more than he walks."

"Okay." She pointed toward the surgery hall. "I'll go this way. Meet back here in five minutes?"

"Yeah." I squeezed her hand and watched her walk away in a pair of green capris-length jeans with pockets made with flower patterned cloth sewn on the side and permanent dirt stains on the knees. The blue and white plaid shirt tucked into the high-waisted pants emphasized her hips and gave me a magnificent view of her ass. A growl rumbled in my chest as my wolf whispered, 'mate.' Once she was out of sight, I walked down the outpatient surgery hallway.

At 5 a.m. few people walked the halls, and none looked up as they passed me. The entire place smelled of antiseptic and a mush of human smells. Every now and then I'd catch a hint of a shifter. As I moved down the hall, the scent of a bear shifter caught my nose. I followed it. He might know my brother.

I turned the corner and saw a large man with a bushy beard in a set of green scrubs. He wrote on the clipboard he held. His nose twitched, and he looked up.

"I have many questions." He raised an eyebrow at me.

"Good. Me, too. I take it you know Flynn Curran?"

"Yes, I do."

"I need to find him. And quick."

At that moment, Flynn ran around the corner dressed in light blue scrubs. His hair looked longer than ever, and he now had a short beard. "What are you doing here? You can't be here."

"Too bad. I need your help." I sighed. If only I could see him under better circumstances.

"No, you don't. I won't go back." His wide eyes burned with anger.

"Just for a few hours. Please."

"Excuse me," the large man said. "What's going on?"

"Hugh, this is my sister, Tessa. She wants me to go back home." He rolled his eyes at me.

"Hi, Tessa. I'm Hugh and I can't let you take Flynn back to where he grew up."

I ignored the bear, crossing my arms over my chest. "Dad didn't name a successor, and Blake is starting a war.

Do you think he's going to leave you alone?"

"He won't be able to find me."

"Not at first, but if he looks for you, it won't take him long." I knew there wasn't much I could say to convince him to trust me and it hurt the worst.

Flynn rolled his eyes. "I'm not afraid of Blake."

"Well, I was attacked by four, no, six of his followers on the way here."

"And yet you're still here." He sounded bored.

"I had help."

"Lucas?"

"Nope. A necromancer."

His mouth dropped open. "What? Have you lost your mind? They're dangerous."

"She's the only one who would help me contact dad. And he won't name a successor without all of us together."

"I can't believe you're trusting a necromancer." He hit my arm with the back of his hand.

"I know a necromancer, and she's really nice," Hugh said with a shrug.

"You're not helping," Flynn frowned at his friend.

"Did you find your brother?" Penelope walked up to our group, blocking the hall.

"Yes." I smiled at her, then turned to Flynn.

"Flynn, this is Penelope. Penelope, Flynn."

Flynn's eyebrows furrowed. "Hi."

Penelope waved. "Oh, hey Hugh. How are you?"

"Penn." Hugh leaned down and hugged Penelope. "It's great to see you. So, you're the one helping Flynn's sister."

"Yeah. It's been quite an adventure so far."

I raised an eyebrow at Penelope. "Adventure is a strong word to use."

"It's been a bit of a disaster?" She shrugged.

"I'm still not going home." Flynn crossed his arms over his chest.

Penelope walked up to him and looked him in the eye. "I'm willing to risk your dead father possessing me again. So, you are coming with us, even if I have to enchant you. What's it going to be?"

Flynn backed down and looked over at me. "She's kinda scary."

"She's terrifying."

Penelope hit me. "Well, what's it going to be?"

"It won't be long, and you can leave as soon as it's over," I said.

"What if he says my name?"

"Then you name someone in your stead, as would be your right." I succeeded in not rolling my eyes.

Flynn sighed and shook his head. "I don't know. And I can't leave now. I have surgery in twenty minutes. I'll have an answer by the end of my shift."

"We'll meet you here then. What time?"

"8 at the latest. I would say 7, but I'm covering for someone right now and the changeover might take longer."

"We'll be here at 8."

"Nice meeting you, Tessa. See you around, Penn." Hugh steered Flynn away from us.

I watched him walk away, never looking back. My hope of preventing a full out war lay in the hands of the outcast son.

"What if he doesn't show up?"

"He will." Penelope took my hand in hers and squeezed.

I looked down at my watch. We had a little less than two hours. "Waiting is the worst."

Penelope smiled up at me. "I might know something to pass the time."

She drew me into a slow kiss, then pulled me down the hall. She smiled at me over her shoulder. The deserted hall had one door. She looked around, then opened it, tugging me inside. She locked the door behind her. Dust covered most of the boxes in this unexpectedly large closet.

"We are going to get in so much trouble," I said.

"That makes it even more exciting." She grabbed my waist and guided me behind a set of shelves. Once pushed against the wall, she sank her hands into my hair and kissed me.

I responded immediately. The wolf inside panted and sang 'mate' inside my head. I pulled her close, untucked her shirt, and slid my hands under it, feeling her smooth skin. She sucked on my earlobes and kissed my neck. Her hands wandered down my body, brushing my nipples, then wrapping behind me to grab my bum. She pulled my knee up to caress my thigh. Thoughts of getting caught flew out of my head.

Her mouth traveled to my breast. Teeth pinched my

nipple through the shirt. Her hand moved it out of the way so her mouth could nuzzle and suck on my tit. I moaned.

"Shhh," she said. "No noise."

Then she licked my nipple, and I whimpered. She kissed her way over to my other nipple. I bucked under her when she nipped and flicked it. I bit my lip to keep from groaning. She winked at me. Her devilish grin slowly moved further south. Each kiss and nip on my stomach sent shivers through me.

Her hands pulled down my pants and underwear. A sound almost escaped me when she kissed my mound and rubbed her face in the trimmed curls. She moved the leg she held earlier over her shoulder. Her hands gripped my hips and held me steady.

I trembled when her tongue touched my clit. I felt her hum of amusement before she licked again. Her slow, methodical movements teased me. She circled and flicked at my bud. I ached for her to go faster and harder, yet anytime I pressed myself into her face, she backed off.

"No, ma'am. I want to take my time," she said, then she'd swirl her tongue even slower.

Her fingers lightly caressed my legs and bottom. I gasped for breath when she sped up a little and sighed when she held back. Sweat trickled down my face. I panted, ever grateful for the wall which held me up.

She sucked on my clit, then lavished my vagina. She ate my throbbing pussy, lapping up the wetness. I squirmed and rubbed into her face. Hands gripped my hips harder, and she focused on my nerve center.

Teeth pulled and lips sucked my clit. I wanted more. She licked and flicked faster, only to go slower. I panted harder and harder. Whispers of moans fell out of me. Her hands wrapped around and grabbed my ass as she licked faster and faster. She moaned into me, my body quivering and bucking into her glorious mouth.

My body burned and writhed under her power. I let loose one last moan as I shattered. Her kisses on my sensitive bud made me twitch. She rubbed my legs and kissed my hips. Her hands slid down my legs and pulled up my pants. She kissed up my body.

Her lips tasted like a combination of me and her, earth, coffee, and sweat. My wolf howled inside. Here in this forgotten closet, I could kiss her all day. My hands found their way back under her shirt. I wanted nothing more than to return the favor.

"Hey, you two," a lady yelled.

We pulled away from each other to see a small woman in scrubs shaking a dusty box at us.

"You're not supposed to be in here. Get out."

Penelope looked at me with wide eyes, then grabbed my hand. We ran out of the room and into the hall. We laughed when we found a small waiting room.

I kissed my mate and nuzzled her nose. "We should get cleaned up. Your lipstick is a bit smeared."

"Totally worth it."

She let me pull her into the ladies' room, where we made out until interrupted again.

CHAPTER 13

Penelope

We sat on a hard, black couch in the out-patient surgery area holding hands and whispering to each other. I kept the conversation light, for Tessa's sake. She needed a moment without the worry of her family sitting on her shoulders.

Before eight, we stood in the hall where I met her brother. She tapped her foot and checked her watch. Each passerby caught her attention.

At five past eight, she sighed and leaned against the wall. "He's not coming."

"He'll show."

"How can you be so sure?"

"I just am. He'll show to give you an answer, even if it's not the one you want."

She nodded and took a deep breath. She looked up and sniffed the air.

"He's coming." She stood up straight.

Her brother glided toward her with Hugh behind him.

Still in their scrubs, they stopped in front of us. Flynn favored Tessa; their eyes and hair were the same color. They even used the same expressions. Flynn frowned and looked down.

"You're not coming," Tessa sighed.

"No. I'm coming. But Hugh's coming with me."

"You can bring the whole damn hospital." She pulled him into a hug.

Flynn stared wide eyed at Hugh, then hugged her back. Hugh smiled and gave me a wink. A weight lifted from my chest.

Flynn pulled away from her, looking between the two of us. "You smell like her."

"There are worse things to smell like." Tessa smirked at her brother.

He smiled at her, standing eye to eye. "I've missed you, Tessa."

"I've missed you, too." Her face softened when she pinched his cheek.

"Let's get out of here." I grabbed Tessa's hand to pull her toward the entrance.

"Did you already say bye to your mom?" Hugh asked.

I stopped in my tracks and slowly turned toward him. "Excuse me?"

"Oh." Hugh's eyes went wide, and he pressed his lips together. "You weren't also here to see your mom?"

Fynn grasped Hugh's arm and whispered, "Don't piss off the necromancer."

"Where is she?" I took a deep breath in an attempt to calm down. Tessa started rubbing my arm with her free hand.

"In room 203," he whispered, and frowned at Flynn.

"Why?" I felt small. Why didn't she tell me?

"I can't say. Confidentiality and all that."

I turned to Tessa, looking down at our intermingled hands. "Do you mind if I—."

"Go." She squeezed my hand. "Do you want me to come with you?"

"I'd like that. Thank you."

She turned toward her brother and Hugh. "Can y'all wait here for half an hour?"

"It's fine," said Flynn. "Go see your mother-in-law."

I turned away before I could see Tessa's expression. I liked the sound of that a bit too much. She followed along behind me, never letting go of my hand.

We made it to room 203. The door created a barrier I didn't want to cross. If I stayed here, it wasn't real. My mom should be at home. She should be at her part-time job. She should be anywhere but here. Hadn't she been through enough?

Tessa kissed my temple. "Go on," she whispered. "I'll stay out here."

Our hands released one another. With one more glance back, I knocked and entered the room.

I walked into the sterile white room with a yellow accent stripe that ran horizontally on the walls. My mom looked up from the hospital bed with a sigh. "Who told you?"

Hospital gowns always clashed with her dark complexion, but it looked worse with her hair pulled away from her face in thick corn rows. An IV ran out of her arm, but her eyes brightened when she saw me. I let go of the breath I was holding. The sight of her in a hospital room without twenty machines hooked up to her eased my mind.

"I saw Hugh downstairs." I sat next to her bed. "What are you doing here and why didn't you call me?"

"It's only a leg infection. I didn't think it was anything serious, but Brody from work insisted I go straight to the ER." She grabbed my hand and squeezed. "He's stayed with me the whole time, and I'm going to be released later today."

"You still should have called." I leaned down and rested my head on her hand.

"I didn't want to worry you. You've got enough going on."

"I'll never have so much I can't take care of you."

"That's 'cause I raised you right." She narrowed her eyes at me. "Why are you at the hospital?"

I glanced behind me. "I was looking for someone."

"And did you find them?" She looked behind me at the door. "Are they on the other side of the door?"

I laughed. "No. His sister is on the other side. It's part of a job."

"Your other job? I can't imagine what coffee emergency would bring you to the hospital. Though if you invented a portable caffeine IV, you'd make millions."

"Portable caffeine IV? I like the sound of that. And yes. The other job."

"You're not fixing to raise all the dead in the morgue,

are you?"

I laughed harder. "No."

"Your magic doesn't help find people. Not living people anyway."

"No, but it's not like I was terrible at hide and seek. Besides, the deceased is being stubborn."

"You've dealt with stubborn before. Remember the dead lawyer that refused to cooperate? You twisted his dead arm, and he gave in."

"He wasn't a shifter." I smiled. Her banter meant she felt good.

"You raised a dead shifter?" Her eyes lit up. "That sounds fascinating."

"It was. His wolf was there with him, too. But he wouldn't talk without all his kids there."

"So you're rounding up the kids. What shifter family is it? Anyone we know?" My human mom loved everything about the supernatural. She told me she didn't even blink when my dad told her about his magic. She immersed herself in the supernatural community, striving to help me make friends and connections, especially after my dad passed.

I scrunched up my face and dropped my head. "It's the Curran family. From the Defolf Pack"

Laughter pulled me from my worries. "I bet the Witch's Council loves that." She grabbed my arm and shook me. "Serves them right for not treating you well."

"Mom, I might have a problem." I leaned in and whispered, "I really like the daughter, Tessa."

"She's the one that's outside the door?" she

whispered back.

I nodded.

"Then do what's right for you, not the Council." Her wide grin helped relieve the tension on my shoulders.

"Do you want to meet her?"

She sat up with a scoff. "Not looking like this!" She looked me up and down and murmured, "I can't believe she'd want someone to see me like this. Girl must be crazy."

I stood with a laugh and wrapped her in my arms. "I love you, mom. I've got to go. Want me to come pick you up this afternoon?"

"No. Brody's still here somewhere."

"You know he's in love with you, right?" I raised an eyebrow.

"I know. I'm waiting for him to ask me out. Call me old-fashioned if you want, but he needs a little backbone if he wants this." She motioned toward her body with a smirk.

"Okay. I will give him the space to woo you." I kissed her forehead. "Call me when you leave. I'll call you when I'm finished if I don't hear from you."

"You'd better call me either way." She shooed me away with her hands. "And bring some of the good coffee beans to the house. I'm almost out."

Before I closed the door behind me, I told her, "I bet Brody would give you some of his good beans."

CHAPTER 14

Tessa

We met back up with Flynn and his friend, immediately leaving the hospital.

The drive to the pack land passed without incident. Flynn and Hugh followed us in Flynn's now charmed car, though we didn't pass any vehicles parked on the roadsides on this leg of the journey.

My shoulders tensed the closer we got to home. Penelope looked toward me every time she heard me blow out a heavy breath. She took my hand and kissed it.

I looked over at her as she drove the old pickup. "You sure you don't want to stay with your mom?"

Her face relaxed into a grin. "Yeah. She has her friend there with her."

"The one with the beans."

She laughed, just like I knew she would. I loved making her laugh.

"Yes. The one with the beans. If all goes well, I can be back at the hospital before she needs to leave."

Her soft hands squeezed mine. I relished in the way her thumb rubbed the back of my hand.

"That's a lot of driving in one day, especially on how little sleep we got."

"Some things are more important than sleep." She kissed my hand again.

I kissed her hand back, then dropped it to braid my hair. Lucas hadn't messaged me since we left. We could be walking into anything.

While I braided, I watched Penelope. She focused on the road while I used my eyes and traced her jaw to her neck and down. The desire to lick her all over had me growling unconsciously.

"You okay?" she asked with a look over at me.

Startled, I tied off my braid. "Yes. I'm good." Heat rushed to my face.

My phone in my back pocket vibrated. I pulled it out and sighed. It wasn't Lucas.

"Do you mind if I...," I asked.

"Go ahead."

"Hey, V." I held the phone to my right ear so I could still glance at Penelope while she drove.

"So what happened? You were supposed to call me." I pulled the phone away from my ear. Veronica could be rather loud.

"Well, I found someone to help. And when she called my father, he said all four of us had to be there."

"That bastard."

Penelope snickered.

"Veronica, you are way too loud."

"How are you going to convince Flynn to come back? He hates y'all, right?"

"He hates our father. And he agreed to come. We are driving to the property now."

"What? I wish I could be there. Can you wait a few more hours before you bring back your dad again?" I could practically hear her bouncing.

"We are not waiting. If you didn't move…" I paused, knowing I'd gotten my point across.

"Yeah, yeah," she whispered. "I have my reasons. I'll tell you one day."

"I'm gonna hold you to it. I got to go. I'll call you later."

"Bye, T."

"Bye, V."

I ended the call and rubbed my face. Penelope gave me a quick glance and tapped her finger on the steering wheel.

"You want to ask something?"

"Yes. But it's not my business."

A soft chuckle built in my chest. "Ask away. If it's too personal, I won't answer."

"Who were you talking to?"

I couldn't stop the smirk. Nosey. Of course, I would be nosey too, but I'm the one who knows we are mates. I wondered if she felt the deep connection as well.

"My friend Veronica."

She turned for a second to look at me. "Is she the one that used to come get coffee with you?"

"Yes. That one."

"I haven't seen her in a while. I thought you might have...uh." She let the sentence fall with a grimace.

"Thought what?" I scooted a little closer to her.

"That maybe you two...uh...broke up." She kept her eyes on the road.

My smirk became a full grin. My mate was jealous. The feeling of joy I got from her jealousy shouldn't be allowed.

"We've never dated. She's my best friend and used to work for me. But she quit and moved away and won't tell me why."

She dropped her hand from the steering wheel and grabbed mine. "Oh."

Sitting with Penelope in the truck, driving down the road, settled my wolf. She panted happily and preened as if Penelope could see her under my skin. The delight I felt couldn't last forever. We passed familiar landmarks. We weren't far from the pack land now. My shoulders tensed up again.

"Are you worried your father will choose Blake?" she asked.

"No." I looked out the window, absentmindedly rubbed the back of her hand with my thumb. "I'll leave the pack if he chooses Blake."

"What are you worried about?"

"I'm afraid of what Blake will do if his name isn't called. He's unpredictable."

"He'll have to abide by the decision. It's the rule, right?"

"Yeah. I'm not looking forward to the change. I'll

either move or adjust to a new leader. You'll go back to your coffee shop. Our fun over with."

"Oh. I, uh. Yeah." She frowned. "Maybe."

"That's what you said, right? Have a bit of fun?" I tried not to stare at her reactions to my words. I wanted to know how she felt before I told her my truth. Could she feel our connection?

"Yeah. I said that. Doesn't mean I can't change my mind." She darted her eyes over to me for just a second.

"Did you?" I held her hand tighter, my heart full of hope. "Change your mind?"

"I think I did." She bit her lip.

My eyes widened; a smile pulled on the edge of my lips. Desire flooded my body.

Before I could say anything else, I noticed our location. "We're here," I said. It was the bucket of cold water I needed to keep myself from asking her to pull over so I could ravish her.

Our focus shifted to the road ahead of us. Flynn and Hugh brought up the rear.

"Here we go. Are you ready to call forth my dad's spirit again?"

"For you? Absolutely."

CHAPTER 15

Tessa

The road leading to the main house was rough on the old pickup. My heart felt heavy. I didn't know what lay ahead on the pack property. Before we reached the main house, two of Blake's men stood in the road. They were the two who followed us into the graveyard. Dylan and Graham. Both big, mindless wolf shifters who followed the strongest, hoping for scraps of power. Penelope stopped the car in front of the two goons. They shifted their weight from one foot to the other and looked at each other.

Penelope rolled down her window. "So, what's it going to be, boys?"

I looked closer and saw bruises and scratches covering their faces and arms.

"We're supposed to stop anyone from entering," Dylan said.

"So, fight it is." Penelope opened her door.

"No. We don't want to fight."

"Then let us pass." She looked at me and rolled her eyes.

"We can't let Tessa pass."

"Well, she's with me. And so is the car behind us." She pursed her lips together and raised her eyebrows.

I smirked. I never thought I'd meet someone as perfect as her.

Graham looked around the car, his eyes widened, and he whispered something to Dylan. They stood aside and waved us past.

"If only it were always so easy," Penelope sighed.

"They're afraid of you."

"I'd rather they respected me."

I rubbed her leg as she drove past. Penelope let out an audible groan at the sight of her car. She parked beside it, which now sat with broken windows, dented doors, and an open, empty trunk.

"They want to stop you from calling back my father. All your summoning tools are gone."

"Bastards. Jokes on them. I only do the ritual for looks. It makes people think they are getting their money's worth." She smirked at me. "You still have the bone?"

I pulled the necklace out of my pocket and handed it to her. We stepped out of the car, with Flynn and Hugh following suit. Lucas rushed out of the tree line from the side of the house, hunched over, looking frantically from side to side.

"Thank god you're back." He gave me a hug, then turned and shook Flynn's hand. "Thank you for coming back. Blake has lost his mind. He's assumed he's in charge. People are scared. Some are packing in secret and plan to get out before he traps us all here."

"That's bad," Flynn said. "I didn't realize he was so bad."

"There's something wrong with him. Always has been. A bit of a narcissist." Lucas rubbed the back of his neck.

"Yeah, but I didn't think he'd grab for power like this." Flynn furrowed his eyebrows.

"I've always suspected this would happen. Just not so quickly." I turned to Lucas. I grabbed his hands. "Did Colt's family get out?"

He nodded. "They went for dinner and haven't returned. Ms. Mary said they were safe."

"Where is Blake now?" I asked.

"He's in the back trying to put the pack 'in order.'"

I looked at the four people who stood before me. "Do we want to go in with a unified force or split up and each take a side of the house?"

"Split," Hugh said. "Siblings go together. I'll go with Penn."

I nodded. Penelope squeezed my hand, then Hugh pulled her around the right side of the house. I led my brothers around the left side. We paused at the tree line.

Blake paced in front of several heads of families. They all hung their heads. Several trembled where they stood. Nico sat on the ground gagged and hands tied, no doubt because of Blake's dislike of his opinions. I clenched my fist and took a step. Red hot fury burned at the sight of the pack in pain and fear. Lucas pulled me back and shook his head.

"Calm and together," Flynn whispered.

Six of Blake's followers stood at attention around the backyard, including the four who attacked Penelope and me behind the diner. I knew Colt followed Blake under duress. It might be the same with the others. We were about to find out.

I took a few deep breaths, then nodded at my brothers. "Follow me."

With my back straight, I stepped into the clearing. "You've been busy, Blake."

He spun on the spot. "You should be dead."

"Not dead. Only inconvenienced. And look. I brought company." I patted Flynn on the shoulder.

Penelope and Hugh still hid in the brush on the other side of the house.

"It doesn't matter. I'm the leader now."

"All four of us are here. We should hear what our father has to say."

"Your witch isn't even here. And if she were, she can't do her spell. Her supplies are out of reach." He looked up.

Overhead, her two duffle bags hung precariously from the branches. I rolled my eyes, then nodded at Penelope. She walked out of the trees with Hugh in tow.

"She's here."

He glanced over at her and laughed. "She's powerless and you know it. Face it, I'm the strongest. I'm in charge."

Penelope held the bone over her head and said, "Jeremy Curran, rise. Come to me and speak the truth."

"You must think I'm stupid." Blake put his hands on his hips and sneered.

The wind whipped around us. Mist congregated around Penelope and in her hair. Near her outstretched hand, the fog formed into our father's face. He rushed Penelope like before, only he didn't gain entrance into her body. He hovered next to her, the upper half of his body and his wolf looked almost solid in appearance.

"Jeremey Curran. Hear the question and speak the truth."

"Ah. The witch. I see you're stronger than you let on." My father crossed his ghostly arms.

"No!" Blake yelled.

"Father. We are all here. All four. Who is your successor?" My voice carried over the stunned crowd.

"All four. It's nice to have my children together once more," he said. "My successor shouldn't be a surprise to anyone. It belongs to the only one who can lead without fear mongering, deserting, or panicking. My successor is Tessa."

"Me?" I looked at Flynn and Lucas. They both nodded at me, as if they knew all along.

"No!" Blake bellowed. "A woman cannot lead. Not without being bonded. And I'm the best. I should be the leader. It should belong to the strongest."

"The strongest?" My father laughed. "Was it strength when you poisoned me?"

A unified gasp echoed over the yard.

"You killed father?" Lucas's face turned red, his fists clenched.

My father looked down at Penelope and sneered. "Unfortunately, Blake is correct. Tessa is the leader so long as she bonds with someone within the week. Might I suggest your mate? You make a good match. Not my first choice, of course. But it will drive Nico crazy."

"I'm going to kill you!" Lucas yelled at Blake. Flynn held him back.

"Good luck with the pack, daughter." My father faded out of existence.

Penelope fell backward onto Hugh. Several of the heads of families looked at me, tears in their eyes.

"No!" Blake yelled. "I'm the leader. Kill her."

Flynn let go of Lucas in time to dodge a fist from Alex. I looked for Penelope. She knelt beside Nico, untying his bindings. Hugh stood beside them, taking down anyone who approached.

I took off after Lucas. He wasn't the only one allowed to take on Blake.

CHAPTER 16

Penelope

I looked up after untying the elder. Blake threw Lucas into the crowd along the back of the yard. Tessa punched Blake in the face, then kicked him in the knee.

All eyes focused on the fight between Tessa and Blake. Blake's men, save one, rushed forward to assist. The outlier started pulling them back. I counted more of them than the six we originally spotted. Hugh followed suit and pulled two of the shifters away from the siblings. Before long, Flynn, Lucas, and the crowd helped. A fight between Blake's men and the rest of the pack erupted around Tessa and Blake.

Two of Blake's men turned away from the fight toward me.

"Where do you think you're going, witch?" one said, rubbing his hands together.

With zero weapons and my bag forgotten in the car, I knelt, sticking my fingers into the ground. I searched for a connection to the cemetery next to Tessa's house. The graveyard lay too far for my grasp, but I found an abundance of animal spirits and bones instead. It would do.

I called on the dead critters. Rising from the earth, I called them to rise between deep breaths. My blood pumped through my body as the vibrations of the animals' spirits flowed around me and out toward their forgotten bones.

The men stalked toward me. Both smirked and rubbed their hands together.

"Attack the two before me." I waved my arms forward.

An onslaught of small skeletons held together with the orange glow of my magic rushed the two men and crawled up their bodies. Tiny bone jaws clamped onto their skin. The men screamed. Limbs shook as they pranced and flung themselves around to get free from the clutches of the skeletal rodents. One ran screaming away from the yard.

The other dropped to the ground. "Please make it stop."

"Who is your leader?" I stared him down, a tiny skull held onto his ear lobe.

"You. You're my leader." Tears streamed down his face.

"Nope. Try again, shifter."

"Tessa. Tessa Curran. I pledge my allegiance to Tessa Curran."

I motioned with my hands. The spirit filled remains dropped from him and joined the larger fight. "Then go protect her from Blake's men."

The fight before me turned into an all-out shifter battle. I didn't know which animals fought for Tessa. I saw mostly wolves, a few cougars, and two bears. The bears worked together, Hugh and the bear from behind the diner, Colt.

In the middle, I spotted Tessa. Her brown coat blended in with the rest of the group, but her white belly and snout stood out. I called for more spirits to join the battle and stayed on the outskirts of the fray. My focus remained on her, my heart in my throat.

She stayed low to the ground, attacking the larger dark brown wolf. Blake. His black snout stood out as well. He jumped on her, leading with his teeth. Agile, she slid out of his path and swiped at his ankles when he landed. He fell after the third swipe of his feet. She clamped onto his back leg and dragged him a few feet. Blood dripped. He broke free of her grasp. The game started again.

CHAPTER 17

Tessa

A battle waged around us, all in animal form. The family heads and my brothers pushed back those still loyal to Blake. Fur lay on the blood-soaked ground. The only one in human form stayed outside of the action.

Penelope. My mate. I smiled. Two of Blake's men flailed about earlier, with tiny animal skeletons attached to their faces. She was amazing.

I couldn't think about her now. Blake and I circled each other, never letting our eyes wander long. His dark brown fur stood on end, making him appear larger. Drops of blood fell down his muzzle where I'd scratched his black nose.

He jumped at me again and snapped his teeth. I swatted his heels with my paws as I dodged. He rarely changed his attack. Charge and bite were enough to take down most of his enemies. I swiftly moved out of the way and nipped at his feet.

He growled non-stop, baring his teeth. I stayed close

to the ground, waiting. He charged me again and turned to follow my retreat. My paw came down on his snout. He barreled through me, tossing me over his body, rolling down his back. As I found my feet again, he turned and swayed left to right.

"Thinking hard, brother?" I asked, using the telepathic link which enabled all shifters to communicate as animals.

A growl traveled back to me. "I will never bow to a female."

"I'd never ask you to bow. I'm not like you."

"Weak willed. It's shameful that you are my sister. You dodge more than you fight."

"You fight like a barbarian."

He ran at me again. I jumped over him. My teeth caught his tail. He stumbled on his side when I pulled him backward. A large black object landed inches beside him with a thud. We both jumped away.

One of Penelope's bags lay beside him. I saw an orange glowing skeleton scamper away from the line which held it in the trees. Those rodents were scarier than the larger skeletons.

Blake used my distraction to knock me down on my side. Exposed sharp teeth leaned into my face. His growl vibrated in my chest. He shifted his weight onto my shoulder. I whimpered.

His laugh echoed in my head. "Weak willed."

I shifted my shoulder, sending his foot sliding to the ground. Rolling away from him, my feet found the earth and pushed me into his side. My teeth found their mark.

I clamped down on his neck, limiting his air supply. He squirmed, and I bit harder. On his back, he had nowhere to move without my teeth ripping out his throat.

"Do you yield?" I asked telepathically to him and to the other shifters around us.

The fighting stopped. Everyone turned toward us. Wind blew through the branches overhead.

"Do you yield?" I clamped down harder.

"I yield." He lowered his eyes.

The surrounding shifters changed into their human forms. Those who fought for Blake knelt, heads bowed.

I lifted my jaws from his neck. Once in my human form, I looked around the group. We all survived the battle. "I hereby banish Blake from this pack for the murder of Jeremy Curran. If anyone wishes to leave with him, I will banish you as well."

Blake rolled over and lay on his belly, still in wolf form.

"You have until sunrise to leave." I turned and looked out at my pack. We all needed medical attention after the fight. I walked toward Penelope, who stood at the edge of the crowd.

Her bright smile lifted a weight from my heart. She looked adorable, with the dirt smudged on her freckled nose. Now the leader of the pack, I'd ask her to be my partner, tell her she's my mate.

Her smile dropped and her eyes, focused behind my shoulder, widened. I pivoted on my heels. Blake leapt toward me, his black snout at eye level. I cursed myself for turning my back on him. I braced my arms for his attack. His weight pushed me down, but I expected the fall, used my back to roll with it, and employed my arms to keep his teeth inches from my face. I applied the momentum from the fall to continue the roll, placed my foot on his stomach, and pushed him up and over me. He recovered from the throw faster than I did. Large paws dug into the dirt and rushed my way again just as I picked myself off the ground.

Before he reached me, a large black object landed on his head, stopping him in his tracks. He laid on the ground. The large black object rolled off his head.

Penelope's second bag. I looked at her. Her mouth hung open and her eyes the size of saucers. She looked at me, then we both looked up at the trees. A single skeletal critter hung from the line, which held the bag in place. It chattered its teeth together.

Penelope waved her arm at it. "Off you go. Rest again, my friend."

Nico rushed over and checked Blake. "He's dead."

I sucked in a deep breath. "Are you sure?"

Nico looked up at me with a frown. "Yes. What was in that bag?"

Lucas unzipped it and pulled out the cauldron.

Penelope's face fell. "I'm so sorry."

"You have no reason to be sorry. It saved me." I squeezed her shoulder.

"Tessa, we need to stop everyone's bleeding," Flynn said.

I looked at my pack, then at Penelope. "I'll be right back."

She nodded and smiled. I hated to leave her. I had so much I wanted to say, but the pack needed me to help them heal in more ways than one.

I went around to the pack members and helped with the wounds. Most had questions about the future of the pack. I answered as many as I could. When asked about my partner, I told them I'd make an announcement later in the day. My work didn't end there. I talked to Nico about we would handle Blake's death, especially since he died in wolf form. The older pack members approached me and pledged their allegiance. The men who followed Blake did the same, all impressed with my fighting skills.

I felt sick to my stomach after seeing the death of my brother. We didn't get along, but I never wanted him dead. I needed Penelope to wrap my arms around her. I turned to find her as I walked among the throng of shifters, but I couldn't find my mate.

"Hey, Lucas. Have you seen Penelope?" I asked.

He turned and nodded. "Yeah. She left about an hour ago. I told her you'd bring her a check later."

I grabbed his shirt. "What else did you tell her?"

CHAPTER 18

Penelope

My heart raced. As someone connected to death, I'd never seen someone die right in front of me. Tessa's touch calmed me, but all too soon she left to check on the wounded. I helped those I could. Many waited to speak with Tessa after their wounds began to heal.

I naturally looked for her through the crowd as I helped her pack. When our eyes met through the small crowd, we smiled. This pack would be alright. Tessa demonstrated a desire and strength needed to lead them. As she checked the wounds on each person, she talked to them. I watched her listen and smile at each one. She never rolled her eyes or let them see her exhaustion.

It seemed strange I'd only really known her for one day. I felt comfortable around her. But I remembered her father's words. She could lead, but only if she bonded with someone. He said she had a mate. She distinctly told me she didn't. Why would she lie? And why would she knock on my door if she had a mate?

I didn't know enough about shifters to understand how they found their mates or if it should be a secret from outsiders. With a sigh, I walked to my bags, both abandoned in the yard. I picked up the lighter bag and saw Lucas near the other.

"Lucas. Do you need to keep the bag for evidence?" I didn't know how they would handle a death on pack land either. They couldn't call the local sheriff's office.

"No. You can take it." He smiled. "Thank you for your help."

"No problem. It's the most exciting thing I've done in years. I'm glad I could help."

"Really though. We're indebted to you. I'm sure you'll be invited to the official ceremony when Tessa is recognized as the leader."

"That'd be nice. Is it a black-tie affair?"

He laughed. "No. Nothing that fancy."

"So, how is it going to work? She has to bond with someone. What does that mean?" I picked at the hem of my shirt. It became untucked during all the excitement.

"It's like getting married, only more permanent. Dad said she should pick her mate. She never let on that she had one." He looked over at her across the yard. "She's private like that, though."

"Is she?" I raised an eyebrow and considered what I had yet to learn about her.

"It's probably Colt. Dad said the match would drive Nico crazy."

"Colt?" I couldn't disguise the surprise in my voice.

"He's the bear shifter, right?"

"Yep. They were best friends as children. And Nico will not like a bear shifter being the mate of the leader."

"Oh." I looked across the way to see her walking with him. She laughed.

The reality hit me. I wanted to be Colt, to have her laugh at my jokes. I wanted to be her mate, to support her. I wasn't, though. And why would I be? A witch and a shifter? Not likely. I shook my head but couldn't shake the punch to the gut feeling. She did say that every shifter was different when it came to finding their mates. Maybe it just took her longer to realize it was Colt. I couldn't help but wonder why it couldn't be me.

"Let me help you carry this to your car." Lucas grabbed the heavier bag.

I followed him, feet shuffling to my pickup. I swung the bag onto the bed and looked at my ruined hybrid.

"Sorry about your car. I couldn't stop them." He stuck his hands in his pockets and frowned.

"I'll figure it out tomorrow. I'm exhausted now. Didn't get much sleep."

"You should head on home then. Tessa can drop off the rest of your money later. And if not, you know where to find us."

I looked back at the house. I was a distraction and a means to an end for her. A hollow feeling burned in my chest. "Yeah. Thanks Lucas."

"No problem. Thanks for your help again. You really saved our pack."

I smiled at him and slid into the truck. Tears streamed

down my face when I pulled onto the main road and drove away from the pack, away from Tessa.

CHAPTER 19

Tessa

"Colt?" I wanted to strangle Lucas. "Why would Colt be my mate?"

"Yeah, I already have a mate." Colt appeared beside Lucas with his arms crossed.

"You have a mate?" Lucas said. "Who?"

"Um…" Colt looked down and kicked at the grass.

"Colt. What are you hiding?" I asked.

"She's human."

I sighed in relief. I didn't even know what I was worried about. "I am revoking the no humans rule. If you want to bond with a human or if a human is your mate, I will welcome them into the pack."

Murmurs erupted around us.

"Does anyone have a problem with that?" I looked through the crowd which formed around us.

"You still need to name who you will bond with," Nico said.

"Well, I wanted to speak with the person first, but

since Lucas sent her away, I guess I can't do it now."

"You want to bond with the necromancer?" Lucas's mouth hung open.

"I'm sure she's her mate." Flynn patted me on the back.

I raised an eyebrow at him. "You knew?"

"You aren't the most affectionate person, but you were constantly touching her shoulder or holding her hand. I knew it was more than a crush."

Heat rushed to my cheeks. "Yes. Penelope Solace is my mate, and I would like to bond with her. If she'll have me."

Nico shook his head. "A necromancer mated to the Alpha. And I thought a bear shifter would be bad."

"Is this going to be a long-term problem?" I asked.

He breathed a heavy sigh. "I'm more worried about the Alpha having a same sex mate. It's rare for shifters to have a same sex fated mate. I've never heard of an Alpha with one. How will you produce the next in line?"

"Because procreation is the most important thing? I'm more than a baby making machine."

"No disrespect, Alpha." He lowered his eyes.

"Don't lower your eyes. We can have a discussion. But you're thinking too small. If Penelope even agrees to the bonding, we can adopt. One of us can have a baby, or the next in line will be the child of one of my brothers."

"You're right. Though the Witch's Council will be in a frenzy with one of their own, a mate to the child of Jeremy Curran."

"Somehow, I don't think Penelope will care what the Witch's Council thinks." I smiled at him.

CHAPTER 20

Penelope

Half an hour before closing, I wiped down the tables with the five-hundredth sigh of the day. I almost went home during the morning rush, because of the customers' concern for my well-being. I couldn't hold a smile or even laugh at the bad jokes. Most of all, I didn't have the energy to put on my favorite red lipstick.

Tessa stayed on my mind since I left the pack territory the day before. She'd probably named her mate by now. I left without the check in the hopes I'd see her again. This morning I received a notice saying someone paid off one of my mom's medical bills. One paid off and ten to go. But she paid the bill in full, to the doctor and to me. She wouldn't stop by.

I shook my head. It was my fault. I told her I liked to have fun and didn't have long-term relationships. It didn't matter. Fated mates trumped flings. I wondered if she saw me that way. As a fling. A bit of fun. She'd probably forget me after a while. Here I sat in my coffee shop, and

I still felt connected to her. I never expected to get my heart broken in a day.

"Penn, you okay?" Olivia asked.

"Yeah."

"No one is in the shop. You can tell me."

I sighed and sat down. "I really liked her."

"The lady from two days ago?"

"Yeah."

"What happened? She hired you for your spooky, dead talking skills, right?" Olivia had witches and shifters in her family. I never had to hide the supernatural part of me from her.

I sighed. "Yes. And we spent the day together. She's lovely."

"And you're lovely. Go after her."

"No. She has someone."

She nudged me. "I wouldn't be so sure about that."

I looked in the direction she nodded her head. Tessa walked through the shop's door. She wore her ankle boots, jeans, and an Old Miner's Kitchen t-shirt. She had her hair pulled back into a low ponytail. Her golden eyes seared into me with every click of her boots.

"Hey, Penelope." She smiled.

I swallowed hard, my heart pounded in my chest, and I squeaked out, "Hi."

"I brought back your clothes." She placed the clothes I loaned her, folded up neatly on the table.

"Thanks." I stood up and tripped, falling forward into her arms.

Heat flooded my cheeks. She helped me find my

balance but didn't release me from her arms. We stared at each other, me biting my lower lip.

"Can we go somewhere to talk?" She broke the still of the room.

"Yeah. We can go to the back office."

I took her hand and pulled her along.

"No worries, boss," Olivia called behind us. "I'll handle the store."

I nodded at her, ashamed I'd forgotten her once Tessa walked in the shop. Olivia winked at me and picked up where I left off cleaning the tables.

Once in the office, I let go of Tessa's hand and leaned against the desk. She closed the door, and I heard a soft click of the lock.

"You left suddenly yesterday." She stood against the door.

"You were busy with your pack. I didn't want to divide your attention." I fidgeted with the skirt of my dress.

"Why didn't you stay to get paid?"

I shrugged. "It didn't seem important."

"That money could go a long way in paying your mom's medical bills." She walked toward me.

"Is that why you paid off one of them this morning?"

She smirked at me. "I paid them all off."

My mouth hung open. "Why? How? You shouldn't have. It's a measure above what you owed me."

She held my hands, her face inches from mine. "If I can't use my money to help my mate, what should I spend it on?"

"Wh…what?" I could barely breathe. Did she imply I'm her mate?

"You are my mate." She kissed my nose.

"Your brother said…"

"My brother is an idiot. I want you if you'll have me."

She kissed me before I could respond. I welcomed it. My hands slid into her hair and down her back. She pushed me onto my desk, and settled between my thighs.

A weight lifted from my shoulders as our tongues tangled together. I breathed her in, content in her hands gripping my thighs. She sucked my bottom lip, then let go, her forehead resting on mine.

"I'm sorry. I shouldn't have done that."

"Why not?" I didn't release her from my grasp, afraid of what she'd say next.

"You didn't give me an answer. It's an enormous commitment. And we've only known each other for a short time." She frowned and searched my eyes with hers.

"What are you asking, exactly?"

"I'm asking you to bond with me. To be with no other. To help me lead my pack. I want you by my side. To live with me, to love with me, and to fight if necessary." She took a deep breath. "It's forever. Even if we part, we would feel each other constantly."

I lightly kissed her lips. "I won't sell my shop."

She smiled. "I'd never ask you to do that."

"Can my mom visit?"

"She can move to the pack land if she wants."

"Do we have to live in the main house?"

"No."

"Do I get to see you naked every night?"

She laughed and squeezed my legs. "If you like."

I smiled and rubbed noses with her. "Am I crazy to say yes?"

"Absolutely," she whispered.

"Yes."

She claimed my mouth with hers. I felt her smile against my lips. She rubbed my thigh while her other hand wandered over my back. My nipples reacted to the pressure of our chests pressed together. I wrapped a leg around her waist, pulling her closer. We kissed and bit at each other's lips and tongues. Her mouth traveled to my throat, sucking and kissing me. Shivers rushed through me. I moaned when her teeth nibbled my ear lobe. Her hand snuck under my skirt, caressing my thigh higher and higher.

My hands slid under her shirt, lightly scratching her back with my nails. She shivered at my touch, then sucked my ear lobe hard. The zipper on the back of my dress slid down, exposing my back. Her warm hand massaged me while the other moved to my hip, under my panties.

Her teeth grazed my neck. I cupped her breast while my thumb brushed her nipple, causing her to gasp with each touch. Our lips locked again. While one hand grazed her tit, the other grabbed her ass. I smiled into the kiss.

She pulled down the top of my dress and my bra around my waist. My boob firmly in her grasp, she replaced my mouth with my nipple. I moaned at the sensation. Each tug, nip, and lick sent an electric current straight to my clit, which pulsed in waiting. Her mouth moved to the other breast, sucking on my nipple while pinching the other between her fingers. I leaned my head back. My whole body vibrated.

Her kisses and bites landed on my neck, the hand still brushing and rubbing my hard nip. The other hand pulled at my panties, her fingers getting closer to my throbbing clit.

"May I?" She placed kisses on my lips. "May I touch you?"

"Please touch me." I ran my hands up and down her back.

She pushed my underwear to the side and ran her fingers through the tight curls on my mound. I shivered as her warm chuckle hit my ear. A thumb slid onto my nerve center, rubbing in circles. Fingers slipped into me and her thumb moved faster.

Closing my eyes, I sank into her grasp. I held onto her waist for dear life. Her mouth ravished my neck and my mouth. Sounds escaped me I'd never heard before.

"I want to watch your face as I make you come." She sucked on my bottom lip and flicked my clit.

I bucked in her hand. She smirked, thumb moving faster. I breathed harder, sweat beaded on my brow, and I couldn't look away from Tessa's gorgeous smile.

Her rubbing slowed, then sped up. She drew patterns over my clit, sending shudders through my body. She sucked my lip each time I bit it.

"Oh Tessa, please," I begged.

"Please, what?" She sucked on my neck, the

movement of her thumb steady on my nub.

"Please make me come."

She grinned at me and pinched my nipple. I yelped.

"All you had to do was ask."

Her thumb rolled over my clit, steadily increasing in speed. She licked my lips as I gasped and moaned.

"Oh Tessa. I'm coming." My eyes rolled back, my hands dug into her hips, and ecstasy washed over me.

She held my weight when I collapsed forward. I twitched in her arms as the last of the orgasm uncoiled and she put my panties in place. Our foreheads rested against each other. Her golden eyes stared right into my soul.

"You have no idea how happy I am." She nuzzled my nose.

"You don't know how happy I am that you came back. I thought I'd never see you again."

She wrapped her arms around me. "I'll always come back for you."

"I'll never doubt it again."

"Hey boss." Olivia yelled through the door. "It's closing time. I'm going to leave and lock the door behind me. See you tomorrow."

Tessa and I laughed at the sound of her retreating footsteps.

"Aren't you supposed to have super hearing? It's the third time we've been interrupted."

"You distract me. Besides, getting a taste of you is worth all the interruptions."

I claimed her mouth with a soft, slow kiss. My fingers unbuttoned her jeans. "What do we want to do now?"

CHAPTER 21

Tessa

A week later, I stood on the back porch of the pack house with Nico and my brothers. The entire pack filled the backyard to watch the Alpha Naming Ceremony. Nico would make a speech, and my brothers would acknowledge my role. I could only stare down at my mate, at the bottom of the stairs in her red rockabilly dress, which matched her lips, cap sleeves covered her shoulders, a small bow to the right on her waist, and hose that I couldn't wait to find out if they were held up with garter belt or not.

We'd spent the last week moving Penelope, merging our households, meeting parents, siblings, pack members, and co-workers. Her mom, Regina, loved me, and Lucas couldn't stop hugging the both of us. Flynn decided to not rejoin the pack, but promised to visit more.

When I asked Penelope about the Witch's Council, she told me she told them we were mates and didn't wait for a response. Apparently, she wasn't required to be a member of the Witch's organization, though she'd received a numerous amount of calls congratulating her from witches across North Georgia.

Veronica drove up a few days before to meet Penelope and help me pick out my outfit for the ceremony. Veronica insisted on keeping my outfit a secret from Penelope because it was "fucking romantic." Penelope must have told Veronica what she was wearing, because my red dress matched my mate's perfectly.

During Veronica's short stay, she had a great time telling Penelope all of my other secrets. The more I pouted about it, the more Penelope kissed me as Veronica spun tales about my past. I decided the rewards for pouting far outweighed the embarrassment from the stories.

Now I looked down at Penelope, waiting for the ceremony to end. Her mother stood beside her along with Flynn's friend, Hugh. I suspected Flynn and Hugh were more than friends, but would wait until he told me. Veronica stood in the back, claiming she couldn't stay after the ceremony, so she wanted to be able to leave quickly. I promised I'd visit her soon.

Joy filled me as all the families hugged each other close during Nico's speech with the littlest kids running through the crowd full of giggles.

A cheer went up when Flynn and Lucas grabbed my hands and bowed, placing their forehead to the back of my hands. Once they parted, I held my hand out and smiled down at my mate. Her face lit up, and she practically ran up the stairs, taking my hand. I pulled her to my side, wrapping my arm around her waist.

"Let me officially introduce my mate and the love of my life, Penelope Solace."

The pack cheered louder than before. Penelope covered her face. A faint tinge of pink reached her cheeks. I walked her down the steps to greet my pack as their Alpha.

Once the festivities started, Colt ran up to us and grabbed my arm. "Tessa, have you seen Veronica?"

I looked around the yard. "She said she was leaving early."

"Damnit. I need to explain." He took off running toward the side of the pack house.

Penelope and I looked at each other and shrugged.

The festivities lasted throughout the afternoon. Everyone danced barefoot in the grass, some shifted to celebrate in their animal skin. Nico passed out drunk on the back steps. When we tried to move him, he just pushed us away, saying, "Thank the gods our Alpha is sane."

I had more pressing matters to deal with. My lovely mate looked up at me. I kissed her cheek and whispered, "You look delicious."

She grinned and pulled me closer, only to be interrupted.

Lucas ran up to us and hugged us for the tenth time that day. "I love you both. Thank you for being you," he slurred before Flynn pulled him back.

"Let's get you home." Flynn gave me a wink when I

mouthed 'thank you' before I turned back to my mate.

"So where was I?" My hand caressed her cheek. "Oh yes. You look delicious."

"Look who's talking." She pulled me closer, licking her lips. "Who knew you'd look so good in an A-line dress? How far up does that leg split go, anyway?"

"Patience my love." I kissed up her neck and whispered in her ear, "You'll find out soon enough."

A Bite of Magic Saga
Book 1 - Excerpt

Jesi must find the kidnapped kids, but her magic won't work on the detective in charge. Is he the key to saving the children or the key to her destruction?

Read on for the first chapter of The Witch's Complement, Book One *from the* Bite of Magic Saga.

The bells on the door clattered as it swung open. Jesi pushed inside, closing it behind her. She leaned her back against the door, her eyes closed. The scent of sage and lavender filled her nose, overpowering the other aromas. She inhaled it slowly. The pounding of her heart faded from her ears. Her breathing slowed. She pushed herself off the door, straightened her blazer, and pulled her bag back onto her shoulder. She inhaled once more and opened her eyes.

The store before her was as it always was. Display racks stood on the hardwood floors filled with bags of assorted teas, herbs and spices, gifts, and jewelry. Shelves lined the partial brick walls filled with rocks, crystals, and books. All organized by Maggie, her cousin and the owner, who was shooting quick glances at Jesi from behind the counter.

Jesi gave her a tight smile and began walking toward her. Maggie held her own forced grin as she spoke with the customer she was helping. Maggie's light purple choppy bob blended in with the brightly decorated store. She drummed her fingers on the counter that had books stacked high above her head.

"Thank you so much, Hayley," Maggie said. "I'll be sure to remember that when Roger makes his next order."

They smiled at each other, and Hayley turned to walk toward the door. As she passed Jesi, she gave a fake smile. Jesi veered away from Hayley right before she bumped shoulders with her. She rolled her eyes as the door closed behind her.

"She used to be so nice," Maggie said as Hayley left the store.

"I remember," Jesi said. "What happened?"

"I don't know, but Roger spends enough money for me to ignore her. Want some tea?"

"No. Just a chair," Jesi said, taking a seat behind the counter. "Anyone else here?" She glanced around the empty shop. Her eyes lingered on the door labeled 'The Magic Room'. Anyone not familiar with the supernatural read the sign as 'Employees Only'. Being part of a long line of witches, Jesi saw through the glamor.

"No. Only Hayley and her new tattoo so far today," Maggie said.

"That's why she looked extra smug."

"Yes. Roger did it himself. 'It's runic for Gift. Roger says I'm a gift to the world. But you wouldn't know much about runes'." Maggie's impression of Hayley was spot on. "Looks like a bunch of crisscrossed lines if you ask me. Anyway, what happened?"

"I don't know what you're talking about," Jesi said. She wasn't sure she wanted to share her morning with anyone. She wanted to digest it all first.

"Really?" Maggie said. "You barge in here, slam the door, practically sling the bells across the room, and end up panting against the door. But you don't know what I'm talking about." Maggie looked back at the door. "Were you chased? Did Mr. Fuller's dog get off his leash again? I know Bunny looks fierce, but his name is Bunny and he just wants to lick you."

"No," Jesi said. She leaned back into the chair and looked at the ceiling. How could she explain this to Maggie? Or anyone else, for that matter?

"Then something happened at the police station? What did you find out?"

"Not much." Jesi put her head in her hands. "It's so embarrassing."

"Really?" Maggie dragged out the word. Her southern accent came through. She leaned forward and rested her head on her hands. "Start from the beginning." Jesi stared at Maggie. She knew she had to tell her. But did Maggie have to look so eager?

"You can tell me or you can tell Aunt Sylvia," Maggie added. Aunt Sylvia was the coven leader. Jesi never wanted to tell Sylvia about her fiasco at the police station.

"Fine. I'll tell you." Jesi crossed her arms over her chest. "So, I walked into the precinct. I have my suit on that surprisingly still fits after sitting in my closet for a year, I have my bag, my business cards, and a plan. I walk up to the desk and request to speak to the detective in charge of Aiden Jacob and Pattie Nelson's disappearances. After explaining that I was the families' attorney, they pointed me to two desks on the right side of the room."

"Okay, I'm going to stop you right here and say your suit is on point. Go ahead."

"Thank you. I go to the desk. There I met a Detective Thompson—tall, dark, and pervy. He kept looking me up and down. From Thompson, I learned that they know little about the case. We actually have more information than the cops right now. Also, he isn't really working on it. Detective Chuck Massey is the lead on the case, but his assigned partner just had a baby, so Thompson is filling in when needed. Then, Detective Massey shows up while I'm trying to get Thompson to stop shaking my hand. Massey is tall, blond, blue eyes, and has way too much confidence. Typical detective."

"I like him already. Go on."

"You would. First, I ask if he has any updates. He says no. I explain that my clients want to be in the loop. He pushes back on sharing information and we banter back and forth. I hand him my card, which he doesn't look at, and I shake his hand. And I find out nothing."

"That's it? How is that embarrassing?"

"No. I saw *nothing*. No vision, no past, no present. There was no gleaning. When I shook Thompson's hand, I saw his entire life story. His mom, sisters, the partner he actually works with, how he likes his coffee. I shook Massey's hand and zilch. For the first time in a year, I touch someone and don't see anything." Jesi rubbed her face with her hands. She only got the power to glean a year ago. She saw the past of anyone she touched. Even the briefest of nudges filled her head with a person's history. What if she was broken? Hope filled her for just a moment. She could get her life back.

"Wow. I don't know what to say. Do you think he's a witch, too? But how is that embarrassing?" Maggie's eyebrows bunched together.

"I kinda didn't let his hand go. I actually grabbed on with my other hand. I kept looking from our hands to his face. Back and forth. Back and forth."

"No," Maggie whispered.

"Yes," Jesi said. "I was so flustered. He actually pulled away. My brain kicked in and I let go. I thanked him for his time and I ran out of there. I raced here. What's going on?"

Maggie was looking at Jesi with wide eyes and an open mouth. "Well, there are several, uh, reasons this could happen," she said breaking the silence.

"Like what?" Jesi asked. "You said witch, but I was thinking demon. Or maybe I'm hopeless as a witch and should retire early, then go back to my regularly scheduled life."

"Unlikely," Maggie said. "He could be a witch that has a charm to reject other's magic. What did he smell like? When you touched him, did you feel anything at all?"

"Well, he smells amazing. Like cedar and spring rain. And when we touched, there was a little static and a feeling of warmth moved up my arm."

"Cedar and spring rain? Did you hug him?"

Jesi shook her head.

Maggie continued, "Tell me about the static. Was it

a lot of static? Anything else you noticed in that moment?"

"Normal static, but instead of making me jerk my hand back, I just latched on and I couldn't look away from his eyes."

"He could be a demon. You said his eyes were blue. Did they flicker while you were holding his hand?"

"No. I'm sure. There was something about him I couldn't tear my eyes away from."

"Well, there is a thing, but I want to look into it first."

"Out with it," Jesi said, pointing at Maggie.

"I don't want to give you the wrong idea, in case I'm wrong," Maggie said, drumming her fingers on the counter.

Jesi stared at Maggie. "Out with it," she said again. Maggie had an annoying habit of never being wrong, yet she always second guessed herself. She was a bit of a research queen. Normally, Jesi appreciated her thoroughness, but right now, she needed answers.

"He could be your complement," Maggie said with a small shrug.

"What's a complement?" Jesi asked.

Maggie's drumming stopped. "Really?" She stood up and went into the room behind the counter. Maggie had a workshop there where she put together teas, potions, and spell bags.

Jesi didn't move. She was overwhelmed. She was sinking. Law school fooled her into thinking she would never feel overwhelmed again. Even at her first job as a lawyer at the local law firm, Goldstein, Moore, and Smith, she never buckled under the load. Being the lead on a case for the first time was empowering, not overwhelming. Then a year ago, Jesi's grandmother, Gigi, passed away.

Gigi was a force all her own. She was the leader of the Moonlight Oak Coven. She had respect and knowledge and opened this shop decades ago. Most importantly, Gigi had the witch power to glean. Many viewed this as a dangerous power, to know everything about a person with a single touch. Invasive powers, like gleaning, were only gifted to one witch at a time, or so the old books said. Once that witch dies, it moves on to another one, usually one within a different coven. Often a different country. When Gigi died, the ability to glean, much to everyone's surprise, went to Jesi.

As a kid, Jesi was happy she didn't get a witch power. She and Maggie were the first children in three generations to not develop one. She stopped paying attention to all the coven lessons, not that she had paid much attention before. She grew up and pursued a career. Then Gigi died. When Jesi woke up that day, everything felt energized. Her hair cooperated; all the lights were green on the way to work. She got a good parking spot. She felt vibrant. Then she shook a colleague's hand and everything stood still. She dropped to the floor, flooded with images of his past, good and bad. She couldn't breathe as everyone started touching her, trying to help her up. Asking what was wrong. That was the day overwhelming took on a new meaning. Jesi ran to her office and barricaded the door. She called the first person who came to mind – Gigi. But Gigi didn't answer. Maggie did and came to her rescue. She brought her gloves and a hat, 'just in case'. Maggie was the one who deserved this gift. Jesi thought it was a curse.

Today, she thought gleaning would become that gift everyone told her it was. She could help find the missing children and she failed. It failed. And here she sat, disappointed in herself and delighted at the same time. She felt like the worst sort of person.

Maggie came out of the back room with a stack of books in her arms.

"I didn't know there were books in there," Jesi said.

"There aren't." Maggie put the books on the counter. "They're from the library connected to it."

"I always forget about that room," Jesi muttered, grabbing the book off the top. Old Magik and Companions by Joseph Starland.

"And where are the books you took home last night?" asked Maggie.

"In the car," Jesi said. She turned the page and skimmed. "All I found was a good collard greens recipe."

"Okay," said Maggie, "so, a complement is a person perfectly suited for an active witch, one with a witch power. It's like a familiar that's humanoid," Maggie said as she flipped through the next book on the stack.

"How come I've never heard about this?" Jesi asked.

"Well, for one, you didn't pay attention to the lessons," Maggie said. "And not many witches find their complement. The only pair I know about were Gigi and Gramps. Oh, here is one description. 'If a witch is pure and has the luck of old, she may come across her complement. She will know her complement when her innate power has no effect on the chosen. Complements will become the witch's closest confidant and, in most cases, her spiritual and physical partner'."

"'Spiritual and physical partner'?" Jesi said. "What am I supposed to do? Marry him? What does spiritual partner mean? This is insane."

"Calm down, girl. This book was written in 1200 and translated several times," Maggie said.

"Does that mean none of the spells I cast will work on him?" she asked.

"No," Maggie said. "Your innate ability won't work, so no gleaning. You can do anything else to him... That came out wrong. Besides, we have more books to reference."

"Well, I don't want to reference them," Jesi said. "We have more important things to do. Aiden and Pattie are still missing and we don't know where they are."

"Yes. And if a cop is your complement, we might get the upper hand," Maggie pointed out. "We need all the help we can get."

"What does that mean?" Jesi crossed her arms. Was she expected to charm a cop for his help? Did Maggie want her to put out for the upper hand?

"It means that getting to know this detective could help us find the kids. So, it wouldn't hurt you to learn more about him." Maggie pulled another book and began skimming.

"That's the weakest argument you've ever given

me," Jesi said.

"What can I say?" Maggie shrugged. "I'm tired and not getting enough sleep. I've been scrying, reading, and calling in favors for the last two days."

"Like I said. More important things to do, like pretending you can see into the future," Jesi smirked. "So, why do you want to look into complements?"

"Fine, the psychics are scrying. And my brain needs something it can solve." Maggie looked up, smiling. "So, is he cute?"

"Is he cute?" Jesi said. "That's what you want to know?"

"Yeah. Let me live vicariously through you for a bit."

"You don't need to live through me. You're younger than I am. Go get your own hottie."

"Hottie? So, he's a hottie?" Maggie asked. She wagged her eyebrows and propped her elbows on the counter with her head in her hands. "You mentioned he is tall, blonde, blue eyes, and oozes confidence."

"Never say 'oozes confidence' again." Jesi pretended to retch.

"But he's confident. I bet he has great posture. Did he give a half smile when he shook your hand?"

Jesi raised an eyebrow. "Who are you thinking of right now?"

"Detective Chuck played by a young Daniel Craig."

"I don't need this kind of stress. And what happens if I tell him about all this? He becomes an exposure risk." Jesi rubbed her temples, then moved to her face. She should have kept her mouth shut.

"I'm trying to de-stress the situation. Ten minutes of daydreaming will do us some good. Besides, there is a spell that can erase his knowledge of the supernatural." Maggie shrugged. Jesi squinted at her. How many people has she used that spell on?

"Fine, moving forward. Say this guy is my complement and not an evil witch demon guy, what should I be expecting?"

Maggie looked at Jesi with a blank expression. She then gestured toward the books. "Have books. Will read," Maggie said. "We could always talk to Aunt Sylvia."

"No," Jesi said. "Not yet. I don't want her involved until I have a handle on this situation. Until then, don't say a word."

"You could talk to your mom. And I might be able to put my hands on Gigi's old journals," Maggie said. Jesi rolled her eyes. Jesi's mom was less involved with the coven than Jesi and she'd had a power for years. She just ignored hers. Jesi's was harder to ignore.

"Journals first, Mom later." Jesi picked up another book. "You know she doesn't like to talk about magic. But you're right. I should call her."

"Oh, here is something else about complements."

"Really?" Jesi stood and looked over Maggie's shoulder as she pointed to the start of the section. "Maggie, you are the best."

"I know," Maggie said, smiling. "Here it says that the witch's active power cannot affect a witch's complement, which we knew. Once a witch meets his or her complement, the complement will see past the magic veil. Complements are a witch's match. They usually stay with the witch for life, either as a friend or lover. And in the case of Jesi Osman, her complement will be her lover." Maggie rolled the r as she said the word lover. Jesi whacked her on the shoulder.

"Okay, let me see that." Jesi took the book from Maggie and started reading through the passage. Jesi just began to feel confident using her power, like she could get her life back together. A complement would derail her progress. Right?

"Do you think there is a section that details how to tell someone that they are a complement and that magic is real?" Jesi asked, frowning at the text.

"Well, you can ask around the family on the 'magic is real' part. Only a handful are married to other witches."

"And no complements?"

"Nope. Just Gigi and Gramps." Maggie looked at Jesi. "So, technically he could be a witch, too, like Gramps. And you are each other's complement. So, let's talk about the part where you gave him your number."

"No, I gave him my card. In a professional manner. And what's the likelihood of a cop you don't know walking in here?"

"Slim to none," Maggie said. "You know I don't do well with cops. You should call him, though. At the station. Wine and dine him. Show him a magical time and get the scoop on the kid's disappearances."

"I think not. You've been here pouring over the volumes. Any idea where those two kids are?"

"Nope. But I know the kidnapper is magical. Once the

first kid was taken, everyone in the coven placed protection spells around their houses and children. Whoever, or whatever, took them knows magic."

"Do you think they're in the community?"

"No. I don't. But some people do. It's causing some rifts," Maggie said.

"Who around here isn't a part of the coven?" Jesi asked. She only knew the witches associated with their coven, even the ones who lived a hundred miles out.

"You'd be surprised," Maggie said.

The bells on the door rang as a customer entered the shop. Jesi's eyes widened, and she dropped to the floor, sitting behind the counter. Maggie looked down at her. Jesi just shook her head, putting her finger to her lips. She hoped Maggie would play it cool. She was a little unpredictable. The last thing Jesi wanted was to visit with Detective Hottie right now.

"Hi. Welcome to Herbs and Healing of Savannah," Maggie said.

"Hi. I'm Detective Chuck Massey," he said. Jesi could hear the old counter creak under his weight as he leaned on it.

"Hi, I'm Margaret Watkins," Maggie said. "You can call me Maggie."

"I'm looking for someone. Do you think you could help me?" His deep voice floated down, giving Jesi shivers behind the counter. From Jesi's seat, she could see Maggie's smile widen.

"Yes," Maggie said. Jesi heard Maggie as she mumbled a spell under her breath followed by Maggie yelling "REVEAL."

Jesi imagined Maggie throwing herbs at the Detective. Some of them floated down on top of Jesi's head. He would arrest Maggie; she just knew it. Maggie performed this spell on several occasions. She liked to keep that combination of herbs on hand to reveal possessed, magical, or other customers. Jesi buried her head into her knees.

"Thank you for the handful of… potpourri," he said. "I'm looking for a Jessica Osman. I believe she works here."

"Really?" Maggie said more to herself.

"She doesn't work here?"

"Oh yes, she works here." Jesi hit Maggie's shin from under the counter. "She's not here right now."

"Well, she left her jacket at the station earlier." Jesi could see the edge of a cardigan draped over the counter next to the cash register. "Also, if she could call me? I have a few questions for someone posing as a lawyer in order to get information regarding an active case. I believe it constitutes as fraud."

Jesi heard him tap the counter and move. Posing as a lawyer? Who did he think he was? Jesi jumped up from behind the counter, red in the face.

"I am a lawyer. With an active license. I have every right to question the progress of the police department on behalf of my clients."

The detective smiled. "I spoke with the people at Goldstein, Moore, and Smith. I hear you took a leave of absence a year ago. Why exactly do you work here?"

Jesi looked at Maggie and then back at the detective, switching from one foot to the other. "I'm helping my family while freelancing. Family comes first."

A C K N O W L E D G E M E N T S

The first version of "The Wolf and the Necromancer" was published in the "Alpha Shifter's Furever" anthology under Naughty Nights Press, LLC in 2022. Thank you, Gina Kincade, for including me in that anthology. I don't think I would have written this story otherwise. That version is five thousand words shorter and was edited by LadyWindsong. "Alpha Shifters Furever" is currently unpublished.

Shout out to my beta readers. They find my many homophone mistakes, let me know where to expand the story, and how to avoid awkward phrasing.

Special thanks to October Santerelli, my original LGBTQIA+ sensitivity reader for this novella.

Thanks to my ARC group. I'm lucky to have found y'all. You're support and enthusiasm encourages me every day.

Did you enjoy this book?

Please review and visit Lucille's website for updates, sign up for her newsletter, and learn how to find her across social media.

www.lucilleyateswrites.com

ALSO BY LUCILLE YATES

A Bite of Magic Saga

The Wolf's Bite
The Witch's Complement
The Wolf's Return
The Wolf's Song

Corporate Shifters

For the Good of the Clan

About the Author

Lucille Yates writes paranormal romance and urban fantasy stories. They feature head-strong women, complicated men, and sizzling chemistry.

Lucille lives in a world full of witchcraft and naps. A recent poll from her sister reveals she's the world's okayest sibling. While homophones create endless problems in her author journey, she still enjoys writing the stories that are constantly playing like a movie in her head. She is excited that others will now enjoy them as much as she does.

When she is not writing, she is reading, playing with her son, watching videos, or playing games. She lives outside of Savannah, GA with her husband, son, and three cats.